"And," Jessica continued, more excited now, if I had my way, I wouldn't even wear a traditional wedding dress at all.

"I'd pick something with a long, flowing skirt. Chiffon, maybe. Lots of flow. Loose, romantic sleeves. Something very dramatic."

"More like a costume from one of your operas?"

"Yes, actually." Jessica felt a sense of relief as the words were spoken. "And not necessarily white," she continued, "which I know would probably upset everyone. But I just see this as a nontraditional sort of wedding—a staged event."

"Right, right."

"I'd like to see a little color, even in my gown. Muted, of course. If we're going with a Mediterranean theme."

"*Are* you going with a Mediterranean theme?"

"Well, I've tried to tell Nathan my ideas, but he's got a more traditional approach in mind. Not that he's being stubborn. He's not." Jessica drew in a deep breath. "He's almost too nice about it all, but I can see it in his eyes. He's very 'in the box'—which is fine. That's just who he is, and I appreciate that about him. He's solid, stable."

"Romantic?"

"Well, I can't expect everything from one person," Jessica said slowly. "But I'm fine with that. I really am."

"Humph."

"Besides," Jessica said, trying to turn the conversation in another direction, "I don't want to hurt him by insisting on having my own way. That would be wrong. And I'm more than willing to compromise."

"Your wedding plans, you mean?" Another penetrating gaze.

"Of course. What else would I be compromising?"

Her grandmother's wrinkled brow alarmed her. "You're a wise girl, Jess. And I know you'll make the right decision."

JANICE THOMPSON is a Christian author who resides in south Texas with her husband and four daughters. Her entire family is active in their local church and in inner-city missions. They spend much of their time working with Houston's homeless community. Together they hope to make a difference by bringing the love of Christ to a generation of young people who simply need a helping hand.

Books by Janice Thompson

HEARTSONG PRESENTS
HP490—A Class of Her Own
HP593—Angel Incognito

Don't miss out on any of our super romances. Write to us at the following address for information on our newest releases and club information.

Heartsong Presents Readers' Service
PO Box 719
Uhrichsville, OH 44683

Or visit www.heartsongpresents.com

Pretty Good Story
Fast Read

Janice A. Thompson

AUTHOR

A Chorus of One

TITLE

DATE

This melodic tale is dedicated to my very "vocal" daughters—Randi, Courtney Rae, Megan, and Courtney Elizabeth. (Yes, I really have two daughters named Courtney!) The Lord has truly gifted each of you for His purpose, and I'm thrilled to watch you step into the roles to which you have been called. Recognizing and developing your God-given artistic gifts has positioned you to discover your "use-ability" within the body of Christ. Remember—as long as you continue to keep your hand in His, you will never be "A Chorus of One."

A note from the Author:
I love to hear from my readers! You may correspond with me by writing:

Janice Thompson
Author Relations
PO Box 719
Uhrichsville, OH 44683

ISBN 1-59310-126-0

A CHORUS OF ONE

Our mission is to publish and distribute inspirational products offering exceptional value and biblical encouragement to the masses.

Or check out our Web site at www.heartsongpresents.com

one

"That's it! That's the one." Jessica Chapman let out a squeal of triumph as her gaze fell on the most beautiful wedding invitation imaginable.

Her fiancé, Nathan Fisher, looked up from the book of samples, clearly stunned. "The beige one?"

"It's not beige, Nathan. See?" She pointed. "It's cream linen." Jessica spoke with dramatic flair then leaned down for a closer look. "Besides, there's a lot of color in this exquisite lettering. Don't you just love all of the detail?"

"I guess." He shrugged.

"But you know what I love most about it?" She reached down to run her finger across the embossed print. "The European design reminds me of *La Bohème*."

"Let me guess—an opera, right?"

"Not just an opera." Jessica's voice swelled with excitement. "It's an amazing love story about a young woman who dies in the arms of the man she loves. Tragic, really." Tears sprang to her eyes, and she quickly brushed them away so that Nathan wouldn't poke fun at her.

"Uh-oh. Here we go again."

Jessica pulled her hands to her chest and sighed deeply. Could she help it if she loved the theatrical?

"The way things are going, we might as well sing this whole wedding." Nathan looked up with a playful smile. "That's what I'd call tragic."

"Very funny." She jabbed him in the ribs, and he doubled over, pretending to be in pain. Nathan had often accused her of turning this wedding into a production, but that's what the most special day of your life should be, after all. Surely he would grow to understand her sense of style, even appreciate it.

"Problem is," he continued, "I'm tone-deaf, as you well know. So singing our vows is out of the question. Unless you give me a few voice lessons between now and then."

"I'm not sure lessons would do much good, all things considered."

"Oh, you're a laugh a minute."

"But really." She turned back to the book. "What do you think of this invitation? I just love the fancy print." She ran her finger across the raised letters with their curly edges. "It looks so elegant. And see how reasonably priced they are? They're definitely within our budget."

"If that's what you want, I'm fine with it." He turned another page. "But before we make a final decision, what about this one? I really like it." He pointed to a stark white invitation with crisp, gold lettering.

Nathan clearly didn't relate to her overall plan for a muted Mediterranean theme. Otherwise, he would never have given this one a glance. "It's okay. Not really what I had in mind, but if you like it. . ."

"We both need to like it." He sighed. "I just wonder if we're ever going to agree on anything."

He gazed into her eyes with a woeful expression, and Jessica's heart melted immediately. "We both agree that we're in love." She reached up to plant tiny kisses on his cheek. "And we agree that it's the happily-ever-after kind. True?"

He slipped his arm around her shoulder and gave her a tight squeeze. "True. But if we can't even pick out a simple wedding invitation, I hate to think of the trouble we'll have naming our children someday."

"Oh, that won't be a problem." She chuckled. "If we ever have a son, we'll call him Jim-Bo or Billy-Bob."

"Naturally."

"And if we're blessed with a daughter, we'll name her—"

"Carmen Aida Don Giovanni," he said with a wicked grin. "That's a musical name, right?"

"Bravo!" Jess stuck out her hand for a high five. "See? We agreed on something. And you obviously know more about opera than you've been letting on."

He shrugged. "Another thing I think we would agree on is that our daughter had better have your looks and not mine."

"Don't be silly. If she looks like you, she'll be—"

"Tall? Skinny?" He lifted his hands in mock despair.

Jess stood back and gave him a careful look. Nathan was tall, nearly six feet, and a little on the thin side. Years of study had kept him off the basketball court and in the classroom, but she felt no need to complain. He might not have an athletic build, but he looked just right to her, and she wouldn't argue a bit if their children shared his looks. His sandy, lopsided curls always kept her entertained, especially when he attempted to force them into place. As if that were possible.

Nathan brushed his lips against her cheek. "No, she'd better look like you. Those freckles, that red hair. . ."

"Auburn, thank you." Jess groaned. If anything, she felt plain, ordinary—and the hair color didn't help anything. She had always longed for rich, dark hair or even shocking blond, but she'd been stuck with a lackluster shade of red-orange instead.

"Auburn," he echoed, then turned his attention to the book of samples once again. "Now, if we can just get these invitations ordered, we'll be one step closer to the big day."

The big day.

Jess and Nathan's wedding wouldn't take place until mid-May, eight long months from now, but Nathan's classes at the university would begin next Monday. Finishing up his master's degree in financial management would take his undivided attention, and wedding plans would have to take a backseat. That's why getting the details ironed out now seemed critical.

Jess leaned her head against his shoulder, and they continued to look through the samples together. She had adored Nathan Fisher for as long as she could remember. Everyone in high school had known they would someday be married. They were meant for each other. Over the years, her schoolgirl crush had developed into full-blown love. And Nathan had proven his commitment to her over the past few years, walking her through some of the darkest moments of her life.

Jessica paused to think about all she had been through. She still marveled at how the Lord had turned the bad situations in her life around for the better. When her father passed away her junior year of high school, she never dreamed she would experience joy—real joy—again. But so much had come into her life she scarcely knew where to begin thanking God for everything.

Through it all, her mother had proven to be the best example of godliness and strength a daughter could have asked for. Despite her pain, Laura Chapman had done a fine job of caring for Jess and her brother, Kent. This had always made Jess so proud. Her mother was such a woman of God—one who she could only aspire to be like. And the Lord had blessed her mother's dedication, meeting every need above and beyond all expectations.

Jess smiled as she remembered the giddy excitement her mother had experienced two years ago, when the Lord brought a new man, Professor Andrew Dougherty, into her life. He could never replace her wonderful father, of course, but he had been good and kind to everyone in the family and had proven to have an amazing sense of humor. How wonderful to think her mother had found love twice in her lifetime. Was such a thing really possible?

A popular love song drifted out of the store's sound system.

Nathan looked up and pointed to the speaker in the ceiling. "Now here's a song I really like. I definitely think we should have it at our wedding. Or at least the reception. What do you think?"

Jess wrinkled her nose.

"Don't you like it?"

"Well, yes, but. . ." How could she explain that the music she had always dreamed of for her wedding would probably be in Italian? Country music would definitely not be an option. "It's nice," she said. *There will be plenty of time to discuss this later. One challenge at a time.*

"I never knew putting together a wedding would be so much work." Nathan rubbed his brow.

"Me, either," Jessica added. "But I don't suppose we have to make a decision about the invitations today. We've got plenty of time."

"True."

"Besides, we really can't order them until we know how many people we'll be inviting, and we're nowhere near finished with the list." Far from it, in fact. To date, her mother had given her over one hundred names, and Nathan's mother. . . well, that was another story altogether.

"I know my mom's not going to be done with her list for a while." He closed the book.

Jessica sighed.

"You okay?" He brushed a lock of loose hair out of her eyes.

"Yeah." She lost herself in her thoughts for a moment. Nathan's mother had great suggestions for the wedding, no doubt. All of her ideas were wonderful, but a little costly. Of course, Jess would never dream of arguing with her, but wondered if the words "wedding on a budget" would ever be fully understood by all involved.

She appreciated all that her own mother had done so far, and Andrew, in his fatherly way, had surprised her by offering to help, as well. But Jessica felt very strongly that she should contribute as much as possible, in part to pay her mother back for all of the years of sacrifice. Unfortunately, Jess's part-time job at the church barely covered her car payment and insurance, let alone a wedding dress and invitations. But she would manage. Somehow.

"Jess?" Nathan said, bringing her back to the present.

"Yeah?"

"Let's go get some dinner, okay?" he said. "I'm famished."

"It can't be dinnertime already. We haven't even been here an hour, right?"

"Try two and a half hours." He yawned.

Jessica's heart lurched. She looked down at her watch in horror. "It's five forty-five? I'm supposed to be at the Wortham for a vocal audition at six fifteen."

"What? Tonight?"

Her gaze remained fixed on the watch: 5:46. "Yes. The Houston Grand Opera is holding auditions for *Rigoletto*."

"Did you forget?"

"No. I brought my music with me. I just lost track of the time." Jessica had waited for this day for weeks. She felt privileged to be recommended by her college professors at the prestigious Moores School of Music at the University of Houston. If all went well in tonight's audition, she might find her place alongside other mezzo-sopranos in the chorus of one of her favorite operas.

If she made it to the audition.

"Can you get me there in a hurry?" She shot a glance at her watch once again.

"In less time than you can sing an aria."

Jess took his hand and gave it a tight squeeze. "Thank you."

"Come on, Madame Butterfly." He clenched her hand in response. "Let's fly this coop."

Together they sprinted toward the car.

two

Jess leaped from the car and ran across the large veranda of the Wortham Theater. Nathan gave the car horn a couple of quick beeps, and she turned to wave as he steered the vehicle away from the curb. He would be waiting in the diner across the street when she finished.

She pulled open one of the large front doors of the theater and found herself in the spacious lobby. Grand escalators stood in front of her. Jessica glanced at the note in her hand. *Main stage.* She glanced up nervously.

"Can I help you?" A security guard stopped her in her tracks.

"Um, yes." Her shoulders slumped in defeat. "My name is Jessica Chapman. I'm here—"

"For the auditions," he finished for her. "Your name is right here on the list. I was starting to think you were going to be a no-show."

"Am I late?" She glanced at her watch. No, thankfully. One minute to spare.

"Just on time, if you hurry." His smile gave her hope. "Do you know how to get to the main stage?"

"Yes. I'm just a little flustered."

He patted her on the shoulder. "You'll do fine, I'm sure. Just head up the escalator, straight across the lobby, and into the theater. The man you're looking for is a Mr. Gabriel. He's the one with the silver hair."

"Thanks so much. I owe you." Jess sprinted to the escalator and bounded up the stairs, two at a time, not waiting for the slow-moving ride to the top.

11

She entered the auditorium at six-fifteen and was met by a stern-looking older woman almost immediately. "Jessica Chapman?"

"Yes. I'm Jessica."

"I'm Catherine Caswell. Let me introduce you to rest of the panel. Then you can give your music to Karyn, our pianist." Jess allowed her gaze to follow the woman's extended finger to the massive stage where a thin young woman sat at a massive grand piano. She drew in a deep breath and tried to steady her nerves. *I can't believe I'm actually going to sing on that stage. Finally.*

Ms. Caswell took off toward the front of the theater, and Jessica followed in her shadow. By the time they reached the front row, she found herself completely out of breath.

"Jessica Chapman. . ." Ms. Caswell nodded in her direction. "Meet your judging panel—Mr. Gabriel of the Houston Grand Opera, Ms. Venton of the New York Metropolitan Opera, and Mr. Colin Phillips of the Dallas Metropolitan Opera."

"Nice to meet you." She nodded in their direction. Mr. Gabriel never looked up. Ms. Venton briefly glanced up over narrow bifocals, but Mr. Phillips from Dallas extended his hand.

"Just relax, Miss Chapman." He stood and led the way toward the stage as Ms. Caswell disappeared toward the back of the auditorium once again.

Jessica nodded and followed him up the side stairs to the grand stage. From here, she could see the entire theater in all of its beauty. Many times she had seen productions from the opposite viewpoint, but she longed to see the audience from this angle. "I could get used to this," she whispered.

"Excuse me?"

"Oh, I just said I could get used to this." She gave him a girlish grin.

He winked at her. "Then sing your heart out."

She pulled the sheet music for "When I Have Sung My Songs" from her portfolio and handed it to the pianist, who briefly scanned it, then sat at the piano.

Jess instantly realized she had forgotten to give them her résumé. She pressed it into Mr. Phillips's hand. He took it with an encouraging smile.

"Thanks. Go ahead and warm up a little. Oh, and Jessica?" He turned as he headed down the stairs.

"Yes sir?"

"Break a leg."

She felt his calm reassurance and nodded in appreciation. The pianist played a broken chord, and Jessica quickly began to vocalize. Her voice trembled. *Lord, help me. Please.* As she finished the warm-up, she breathed deeply and felt her nerves calm a little.

"Any time you're ready, Jessica," Mr. Gabriel called out.

She stepped to center stage and took one last sweeping glance across the theater before nodding to Karyn. As the music began, she prepared herself, both physically and emotionally. *I've waited for this moment all my life.*

The first few words seemed to stick in the back of her throat, but by the time she reached the chorus, Jessica seemed to feel a little more secure. She looked down at the panel members, who rarely even glanced her way. Only Mr. Phillips looked up occasionally with a warm smile. As she started the second verse, Jessica found herself lost in the emotion of the familiar lyrics. She had specifically chosen this song because it impacted her on many levels, emotionally and spiritually. Her voice, strangely unfamiliar, seemed to leap and dance across the amazing auditorium. By the time the song ended, Jessica felt confident and bold. Almost daring.

"That was beautiful, Miss Chapman." Ms. Venton looked up over her bifocals as she spoke.

"Thank you for auditioning," Mr. Gabriel added. "Results will be posted next Monday on the backstage door."

She nodded and made her way to the piano to pick up her music. "You sounded great," the pianist whispered. "Best I've heard all afternoon."

"Thanks." Jessica whispered her response as she headed for the stairs. Mr. Phillips met her there. For the first time, she noticed more than just his broad smile. He was young, probably late twenties or early thirties, at most. His eyes were lit with excitement, which he wasn't doing a great job of hiding. He extended his hand to help her down the stairs.

"Great job," he said, as she made her descent. "You have quite a range for a mezzo-soprano."

"Thanks." Her hand trembled in his. "Do I exit out the back?" She gestured toward the rear of the auditorium.

"Yes."

She made her way up the aisle with her knees knocking all the way. The security guard met her in the lobby. "Done so soon?"

She nodded, suddenly feeling as if she might be sick.

"You don't look so great. Should I call a cab, or do you have a ride?"

"My fiancé's in the restaurant across the street," she said. "And I'll be okay. Just nerves, I think."

He walked with her to the front door and pulled it open. "Good night, Miss Chapman. Maybe I'll be seeing more of you after tonight."

"I hope so." She shook his extended hand, then made her way across the veranda to the busy downtown street. It wasn't until she was seated across from Nathan in the diner that her stomach relaxed and she finally felt free to breathe a natural, comfortable breath.

"You okay?" He took a swig of coffee and glanced at the television overhead.

She nodded. "That was about the scariest thing I've ever done."

"Did they make you eat a live chicken?" He glanced her way with a smile.

"Very funny. But speaking of chicken. . ." She grabbed a menu and scanned it quickly. "I'm starved. Seen a waitress lately?"

He motioned to get the waitress's attention, and Jessica quickly ordered a chicken club sandwich and fries. Then she leaned back against the seat and poured her heart out to Nathan. He gave her several encouraging hand squeezes and assured her of her ability.

Then, just as her food arrived, Jessica finally let herself think of something other than the audition. "I've been looking at wedding dresses in magazines," she said after swallowing a couple of fries.

"Find anything yet?"

She shook her head. "It's tougher than I thought. If I had a great figure, this would be so much easier."

"You do have a great figure, Jess. Why are you always cutting yourself down?"

She shrugged as she finished a big bite of the sandwich. "I don't know. Just insecure, I guess. Not fishing for compliments or anything, if that's what you're thinking."

"No need." He reached over and squeezed her hand. "You're perfect just the way you are, and I'll always compliment you."

"You're sweet." Jess took another bite then settled back for a relaxing meal. Her thoughts were suddenly interrupted by an oddly familiar voice.

"Miss Chapman?"

Jess looked up to find Colin Phillips standing next to her. She very nearly choked on the sandwich. "Mr. Phillips? What happened? Is something wrong?"

"No, actually. I'm thrilled to find you here. I hope you don't think I was following you. It's just a coincidence, I assure you."

"Okay."

His face lit up. "Actually, I had already planned to phone you at home tomorrow, but this is certainly easier. Do you have a few minutes?"

"Sure."

Colin pulled a chair up to the table, and she quickly introduced Nathan, who then turned his attention to the television for a stock market report.

"Miss Chapman," Colin began.

"Please. Call me Jessica."

"Jessica. This is a little awkward, but I feel like I'm supposed to ask you a question." He pressed his hands together in a tight grip.

Her heart now raced, though she tried to stay calm. "Go for it."

"I'm from Dallas," he explained.

"Right."

"Well, see—we're starting a program in the Dallas area for children. Preteens, mostly, who are interested in the opera. I'm heading up the program. Technically, anyway. But I'm looking for someone who has experience with children to do much of the legwork. This has to be a vocalist, someone who can help train the kids and prepare them for our Christmas production, *Amahl and the Night Visitors*."

Nathan cleared his throat a little too loudly, and Jessica tried to gauge his thoughts. "There's something I need to tell you, Mr. Phillips," she began.

"Please. Call me Colin." The gentleman's rich brown eyes gazed into hers.

"Colin."

She took a deep breath, but he interrupted her before she had a chance to continue. "I forgot to mention that you would also be offered an internship with the Metropolitan Opera in Dallas, which would mean that you would be assured a place in the chorus of both our fall and spring productions. On top of directing the children, I mean."

Her mouth flew open in surprise. "Really? Which operas?"

"*Madame Butterfly* in the fall," Colin said. "November, to be precise. And in the spring we'll be doing *The Bartered Bride*."

"Wow. Two of my favorites."

Nathan shifted in his seat, but Jessica didn't pause for a moment. Her excited thoughts forged ahead. *A place in the chorus. Assured. And working with children to help them develop their vocal gifts. What more could I ask for?*

"Jess?"

Nathan's voice brought her back to her senses. She gazed into his nervous eyes and knew immediately what her answer would have to be.

"I'm sorry to have to turn you down so quickly, Mr. Phillips," she explained, "but we're in the middle of planning our wedding. Nathan and I are getting married in May."

"Ah. I see." Colin paused. "Well, congratulations are in order then." He extended his hand in Nathan's direction. Jessica couldn't help noticing the look of pride in her fiancé's eyes.

"I couldn't possibly leave right now," she continued. "I'm sure you understand."

Colin turned toward her with a penetrating gaze. "Actually, what I'm suggesting would be a six-month internship. You'd be back in plenty of time for the big day. And you'd only be in Dallas, after all."

Nathan cleared his throat again, then shifted his gaze to the television.

"Your voice is unique, Jessica," the handsome young director continued. "And untapped. I could tell from your résumé that you had some amazing opportunities to perform in college, but what I'm talking about would give you the opportunity to train alongside some of the best voices in the country."

"Well, I. . ." *Lord, this is such a wonderful opportunity, but how could I possibly accept it?*

Colin stood. "All I ask is that you think about it. I know this is all pretty sudden, but I've just got a strong feeling God is in the middle of all of this."

"God?" She looked up at him to make sure she hadn't misunderstood.

"Sorry. Forgot I was supposed to leave my faith out of this." He shrugged. "I forget that a lot, actually." He smiled and handed her a business card with his name, address, and phone number.

"It's okay. I appreciate your honesty. I'm a believer myself." Jessica extended her hand, and he shook it firmly.

"Great."

She pulled her hand from his after another penetrating look from Nathan. "Thanks for the offer, Mr. Phillips," she said. "But right now I think I'd better wait and see what my options are here in Houston. I did just audition for a place in *Rigoletto*, after all."

"I know. And one of the better voices we heard all day, I should add."

Wow. "Thank you."

"I do feel like a bit of a traitor stealing you from them, but something in my gut just tells me. . ." Nathan turned an accusing glance his direction. "Well, I've kept you too long. Thanks so much for your time." He left the restaurant in a rush, and Jessica turned her attention back to her fiancé.

"Can you believe the nerve of that guy?" Nathan grumbled.

She wrinkled her nose as she contemplated his remark. "I thought he was nice."

"You're not actually thinking of going, are you?"

"Of course not." She reached over and gripped his hand. "How could I? It's not just the wedding standing in my way—"

"Standing in your way?" A flash of resentment clouded his eyes.

"You know what I mean," she explained. "I've got my job at the church. The kids are counting on me."

"Right."

"And who knows? I might be offered a part in *Rigoletto*. That would be amazing."

He nodded. "That's my girl. Always hopeful."

She nodded and tried to turn her thoughts to her audition, but they gravitated once again. *Dallas*. Amahl and the Night Visitors. *A place in the chorus of* Madame Butterfly *in November*.

"So," Nathan interrupted her thoughts once again. "Tell me about this wedding dress you're searching for."

She looked up into his smiling face.

three

Jessica made her way across the driveway to the mailbox at the curb's edge. She knew she must open it, though she dreaded the news it probably held. Sure enough, the large black box contained the much-anticipated letter from the Houston Grand Opera Society.

She held the sealed envelope in her trembling hand and fumbled with the flap, attempting to loosen it. "Come on. Open up." Then again, why bother? Jessica knew what it would say, even before reading it.

"We are sorry to inform you. . ." The rest would go on to say that while they appreciated her talent and effort, they simply didn't have enough space to give everyone a position in *Rigoletto*. Then they would welcome her to audition again in the future.

These things Jessica knew because she had already seen the list at the Wortham Theater two days ago. Her name had not been on it. She had swallowed both her pride and her disappointment and had given Nathan the news. He had shrugged it off in his usual good-natured way, assuring her of his love, regardless. In fact, he had looked strangely relieved.

But now she must face the letter in her hand. Somehow just reading the news in print would make it seem more real, more awful. Jessica ripped the envelope open and scanned the typed words. Just as she expected. A rejection. She brushed back a tear as she read the words, "You have a lovely voice, and this decision is in no way a reflection of your talent or ability." She shook her head in defeat and wadded up the letter into a tight ball.

"Honey, is everything okay?" Jessica's mother appeared at the curbside. Jess quickly brushed away a tear as she looked up with a numb smile. "I guess." She gripped the paper ball a little tighter.

"Your letter from the Houston Opera?"

"Uh-huh. But at least I knew ahead of time." She sighed deeply. "It's no big surprise."

"I know." Her mother's brow wrinkled in concern. "But I'm really sorry, honey. You've got such a beautiful voice, and I know the Lord is going to use you to minister to others with that gift. I guess this just wasn't the right time."

"Or the right place." Jessica fought to swallow the ever-growing lump in her throat.

"There will be plenty of operas in your future." Her mother placed her arm around Jessica's shoulder. "And in the meantime, you've got a lot of work to do with the children's choir at church, right?"

"Right." But that didn't lessen the pain of rejection she felt in this moment.

Her mother patted her on the back. "The kids need you, honey. And so does Mrs. Witherspoon. She wouldn't know what to do if she lost you."

Jessica didn't know how to respond. The elderly Mrs. Witherspoon, truth be told, had a knack for dealing with the children. In fact, she could take charge of the whole thing in a heartbeat, if need be. But right now Jessica needed to be needed.

Somewhere.

She reached to close the mailbox and looked up into her mother's kind eyes. "Do you think maybe God is trying to tell me something?"

"What do you mean?" Her mother looked concerned.

"Well, I know I'm supposed to be singing classical music," Jessica explained. "That's what I've trained for. But there's not much opportunity at church for that sort of style. So the opera has always been my goal."

"Right."

"I'm just wondering. . . ." She paused.

"About the position in Dallas?" Her mother seemed to read her thoughts.

"Uh-huh." Relief washed over Jessica. "I mean, doesn't it just sound like God had the whole thing set up in advance?"

"It would be a marvelous opportunity." Her mother walked alongside her as they approached the house. "But whether it's in the Lord's plan is another thing. Just because something is easy doesn't always mean it's from the Lord."

"I guess." Jessica heaved a sigh. "But how will I know unless I try it?"

Her mother stopped and looked her in the eye. "You're actually thinking of going to Dallas in the middle of planning a wedding?" She gave her a curious look.

"I don't know, Mom. I'm just thinking out loud."

"Does Nathan know you're considering this?"

"No." She pulled the front door opened and stepped inside. "I'm afraid to talk to him about it at all, to be honest. He's so busy with his new classes and seems a little distracted. But it's such a great thing they're doing up there." She paused then looked at her mother for a bit of encouragement.

"Well, pray about it, honey. God will show you what to do."

Jessica's shoulders slumped as she crossed the house to her bedroom. She tossed the letter in the trash can right away, determined to put the whole thing behind her. Then she reached into her bedside drawer and pulled out another letter—one she had received just yesterday, in fact.

A letter from Mr. Phillips. A "just in case" move on his part, or so it had said. In his carefully crafted note, he had formulated a plan for the internship, offering Jessica a "creative, interactive, and educational environment in order to promote and develop an appreciation of opera as an art form; to provide educational opportunities for all ages and cultures; and, therefore, to supply the opportunity for lifelong learning." He described the youth apprentice artist program in a way that had intrigued and excited her.

Twenty exceptional artists will be selected by vocal audition from applicants from the Dallas Metroplex. Each young artist selected will be given many of the skills necessary for a professional career. The program director will assist each child by providing personal attention and instruction, and significant performing opportunities. These artists work with a team of highly experienced professionals and will receive coaching in standard operatic repertory. They will also be offered multiple performance opportunities.

Jess stretched out across her bed with the letter in her hand. "It almost sounds too good to be true." But how could she balance this against her wedding plans? Would Nathan think she had lost her mind?

Her thoughts gravitated to her fiancé. He was so sweet—and such a good guy. She had always appreciated and loved his understanding heart. While he clearly didn't share her love for the opera, he had never discouraged her from following her dreams. Perhaps he would begin to see this possibility as a part of God's plan for her life, her future.

"Only one way to know for sure." She picked up the telephone and dialed his cell number. He didn't answer until the fourth ring. When he did, his voice sounded hushed, strained.

"Hello?"

"Nathan, is that you?"

"I'm in the middle of class right now," he whispered. "I forgot to turn off my phone. Everyone's looking at me."

"Oh, I'm so sorry. Call me later." She quickly hung up and

shook her head in despair. "Great."

A tap on the door interrupted her thoughts. "Come in."

Her mother entered. "I just wanted to let you know that Andrew and I hoped to take you and Nathan to dinner tonight. We were thinking of that new seafood place up in The Woodlands. Sound good?"

"Very." Her mouth began to water, just thinking about it. "But I'll have to get back to you about Nathan. He's in class right now."

"Okay, honey. We just thought it would be a good time to discuss plans for the wedding—get a few things down on paper."

"Sounds good."

Her mother left the room, and Jessica rolled back over on the bed. Within minutes she fell into a deep sleep. She dreamed of *Amahl and the Night Visitors*—the hauntingly beautiful Christmas story. It seemed strangely twisted into the plot of *Madame Butterfly*, which made for a colorful, yet confusing, dream. She played the role of the beautiful young Japanese woman in love, betrayed by the man who had captured her heart. Just as she stepped to center stage to sing her big solo, Jessica heard the sound of a familiar voice.

"Wake up, sleepyhead."

She propped herself up on her elbow and squinted up at Nathan, who stood in the doorway with a grin on his face.

"What time is it?" she asked with a yawn.

"It's five forty-five. You called me at two o'clock."

"No way." She rolled over to look at the clock.

"Is it okay to come in?"

Jessica nodded, and Nathan stepped into the room. "Your mom called me about an hour ago to ask if I wanted to go out to dinner with you guys," he said. "So I'm here."

"I can't believe I slept all afternoon." She yawned again and sat up. As she did, her letter from Dallas fell to the floor.

"What's this?" Nathan reached down to pick it up. "Your rejection letter?"

"No, I uh. . ."

"Your mom told me it came today." He gripped it tightly. "She figured that's why you needed the sleep, to recover from the bad news."

"Uh, no." She snatched it from his hand. "It's, uh. . ."

A worried look crossed Nathan's face.

"It's just a letter from—"

"That guy from Dallas?" Nathan asked.

"Yeah. But he's not actually back in Dallas yet. He's going to be in Houston for another couple of weeks."

"I see."

"There's nothing to see, Nathan."

"He just won't take no for an answer, will he?"

Jess shrugged. "Actually, I've been thinking—"

"There's nothing to think about." Nathan reached out and took her hand. "He can't have you."

"But—"

"You're a Houston girl, and you're all mine."

She nodded and let her head fall onto his shoulder. As he stroked her hair, he continued. "And speaking of being all mine. . ."

She looked up into his eyes, which twinkled merrily. "What?"

"I have some good news. But let's go out into the living room so I can tell everyone at once."

Jess quickly touched up her lipstick then met them in the living room. There, Nathan gathered the whole family around him to make his announcement.

"I have some news." He paused momentarily, then proudly announced, "My parents have decided to spring for a European honeymoon."

"Europe?" Jess immediately began to weep. She had always

longed for a trip to Italy. For years, she had talked of it with such longing. Venice would be the destination of choice. And Florence, of course. There were so many places to visit, so many historical and musical sites to take in.

But why would Nathan's parents go to such trouble? They must have been listening to her childish babblings all along. Suddenly she felt completely overwhelmed at their generosity. "That's the sweetest thing I've ever heard," she whispered.

"I thought you'd like it." He smiled. "My mom has a friend who's a travel agent, and they set the whole thing up today. We'll fly into Frankfurt."

"Germany?" *That's curious.*

"Yes, I've always wanted to take a boat trip down the Rhine. Then we'll go on to Paris and London from there."

"Paris and London?" That all sounded great, but how did Italy fit into the plan?

"A fabulous ten days of sightseeing and exotic foods for my new bride. British tearooms, double-decker buses. . . The best."

Laura and Andrew immediately began to chatter about French foods, and Jessica's brother, Kent, overlapped them with a conversation about German automobiles. Nathan tried to keep her attention by telling her about their flight, their hotels, and their detailed schedule, but Jess felt lost in the muddle of it all.

Somehow, Italy had slipped right through her fingers, and she felt the loss more acutely than a rejection letter from Verdi, himself.

four

Jessica spent the following Saturday afternoon making a to-do list for her wedding. She tried to push all thoughts of Dallas as far away as possible. With so much planning ahead, she shouldn't have much difficulty pressing misguided images of *Madame Butterfly* out of her mind.

"Photographer. Invitations." She mumbled aloud as she wrote. "Flowers. Candelabra. Roman columns." She paused a moment before erasing the last entry. Nathan would never agree to Roman columns, in spite of her best explanations and pleas. "Buffet, vegetable trays, quiche. . ."

Jessica continued to write, scribbling down only the things she knew the two of them together would come to agreement on. After some time, she laid down the lists and reached for a bridal magazine. She thumbed through it in bored silence as she carefully examined each dress. To be honest, they all looked the same to her. *White with long train. White with short train. Beaded with short sleeves. Beaded with long sleeves.* Did it matter anyway? They were all dreadful. Would she ever find one that appealed to her?

Jessica's eyes grew heavy as she turned the pages. In her mind's eye, she could see her gown. It would be so different from anything in these magazines. So vastly different. She rested back against the sofa and tried to stay alert, but it grew more difficult. For some reason, every time she tried to focus on wedding plans, she grew weary with the process almost immediately.

Jessica allowed herself to contemplate something else for a moment. *Just a minute or two of dreaming won't hurt.* In her mind's eye, she saw herself on a stage, singing her heart out. She wore an exquisite, flowing dress in shades of cream and burgundy. To her left, a beautiful set filled the stage—an antiquated Italian city with houses, fountains, and cobbled streets. From inside the window of one of the houses, a man sang to her in a rich baritone voice, which resonated across the theater.

She responded to his words in Italian. Her soprano voice paralleled his, as they joined together in harmony to complete the song. He disappeared momentarily, only to reappear in the doorway of the house. The tall stranger with dark hair moved toward her, never taking his gaze off of hers. He swept her into his arms and sang lovingly to her, as he danced her across the stage. She found herself captivated by the moment and completely lost in his gaze. They seemed to mirror each other perfectly.

As if anything could be that perfect.

"I've got to stop this." Jessica tried to shake off the image. She tossed the bridal magazine onto the coffee table and stood with a yawn. Enough with the dreamy schoolgirl imaginations. Life was staring her in the face, and she had work to do. Lots of work.

And yet she didn't feel like working on the wedding. She wanted to think about—dream about—singing. *Why, Lord? I thought my life was settled. I really thought I could have it all— the husband, the family, and the music. Was I wrong, Father? Show me what to do.*

The telephone rang, startling her. Jessica felt her hands begin to tremble as she picked it up. *Don't read too much into this.* "Hello?"

"Jess? Is that you?"

Her heart lifted as she heard Nathan's voice. "Yep. What's up?"

"Just wondering what you're up to."

"Oh. I—I was just sitting here making plans for the wedding."

"Good girl." He paused. "Listen, my parents were wondering if you wanted to come over for dinner. My mom's fixing lasagna and Caesar salad. I know they're your favorites."

Jessica's mouth watered. "Mmm."

"And I think she's nearly finished with her guest list for the wedding, and she'll want to talk to you about that. She needs to feel wanted, if you know what I mean."

"I do."

"Also, my dad's been on the Internet again," Nathan said. "He's printed up some pictures of the hotels we'll be staying at on our honeymoon. He's anxious to show them to you."

"What time should I be there?"

"Six thirty?"

She glanced at her watch. "Sounds good. Gives me just enough time to take a quick shower and change into clean clothes. I'll see you then."

"Great. Love you, babe."

"Love you, too." She hung up the phone with a click and picked up the bridal magazine for one last glance. *Lord, is this Your answer to my question?* Though she still didn't feel completely settled on the issue, the phone call seemed entirely too coincidental.

As Jessica climbed into the shower, she finally felt some sense of resolution on the matter. She loved Nathan. He loved her. She had a lot of work to do right here in Houston. Everyone needed her. There would be plenty of time to think about her career later. Timing was everything, after all. Her favorite scripture from Ecclesiastes reminded her of the fact. *There is a time for everything, and a season for every activity under heaven.*

This simply wasn't the time for leaving.

By the time she finished dressing for dinner, Jessica knew what she must do. She reached for Mr. Phillips' letter one last time, scanning it only briefly to find his cell number. Once located, she picked up the phone and dialed it. She would give him her answer.

Her final answer.

&

Colin sat on the balcony of the downtown Houston hotel, drinking in an unexpected evening breeze. From inside the room, his cell phone rang, rousing him from a near-catatonic state. He sprinted inside. Just as he approached the phone, Colin stubbed his toe on the sharp edge of the dresser. He began to hop up and down, then grappled to pry the flip phone open before he lost the call altogether. "Hello?"

"Mr. Phillips?"

The female voice sounded oddly familiar. Colin placed his aching foot back on the ground and winced in pain. "This is he."

"Oh, hello. This is Jessica. Jessica Chapman. We met last week."

His spirits lifted immediately, and his foot suddenly felt better. "Jessica, it's so good to hear from you. You got my letter then." He had taken a chance by sending it, to be honest. In fact, he had prayed the carefully crafted note wouldn't seem too forward, too pushy. But he knew in his spirit this girl was the one he had been praying for.

For the internship, of course.

"Yes. Well, that's why I'm calling." She hesitated. "I hope I'm not interrupting anything."

"No. As a matter of fact, I'm still here in Houston. I've been in meetings all week, but I'm back at the hotel now."

"Ah. Well, I'm glad I picked the right time to call," she said.

"With good news, I hope." He drew in a deep breath and waited for her response.

"Actually..."

Colin's heart suddenly felt heavy. He dropped down onto

the sofa to await her reply, rubbing his aching foot as she spoke.

"I've really given this a lot of thought," she said. "And I've prayed about it, too. But—"

He switched the phone to the other ear. "You've decided against it?"

"I'm afraid so."

She sounded as if she would cry, and Colin suddenly realized the struggle she must be facing. "I'm sorry to hear that," he said.

"There's just so much going on right now," she continued, "and leaving in the middle of everything would present too many challenges."

Colin struggled with his disappointment but quickly opted to do the right thing, for her sake. "Jessica, thank you so much for calling," he said. "And thanks for considering the internship. I knew from the get-go that your answer would probably be no, but I was so taken with your voice and your love for children that I couldn't help pursuing it. To be honest, I was only thinking of what you could do for us, how you could benefit our organization—not the other way around. That was selfish of me, and I'm really sorry if I've been too pushy."

"Oh no," she said. And then her voice broke. "I–I'm so flattered you would think of me. It means so much to hear your kind words, and I know the Dallas Metropolitan Opera could have opened great doors for me. Just the opportunity to perform with such amazing professionals in the field—"

"Yes, well."

"I'd honestly love nothing more than to come," she said with a sigh. "In my heart, I'm there already."

"You don't have to say anything else," Colin interrupted. "Just please know this, in case you ever doubt it. You have a unique voice, a God-given talent. And there will be plenty of opportunities for you in the music world. Promise me you won't ever give up on that gift, okay?"

"Okay." She practically whispered the word.

"And if your situation changes in the next few weeks. . ." No, he wouldn't say it. He didn't want to be guilty of manipulating her in any way. Besides, the Lord had the perfect person in mind for the job, and Colin didn't want to interrupt the Almighty's plans.

Even if it meant losing the one person he had felt so strongly about from the very beginning.

five

"What do you think of this one, Grandma?" Jessica turned in a prissy circle to display the white Cinderella-style wedding dress she wore. The romantic gown with its long, full skirt and fitted bodice accentuated her waistline, but something about it still didn't feel quite right.

"Hmm." Her grandmother, never one to mince words, crossed her arms and gave Jessica a penetrating look. "Turn around one more time, so I can give it a fair analysis."

Jessica swished the elaborate gown as she pivoted once again.

"I don't know, honey." The silver-haired woman shrugged. "Something about this one just doesn't seem to suit you. I don't want to burst your bubble. If you like it, that's all that really matters."

"I like it." Jess looked in the mirror once again. "But I don't *love* it; you know what I mean? I want my wedding gown to be perfect. This is close, but—"

"Not quite the right fit?"

"Nope." She shook her head and gave a defeated sigh. "None of them seems to suit me and, to be honest, I just don't know how many more of these I can try on. I'm so frustrated. The last one made me look like a ballerina. That tulle skirt was just too much. Felt like a tutu. And the one before that—"

Her grandmother laughed. "I know, I know. Made you feel like a prom queen."

"That shiny fabric made me a little nervous." She swished in front of the tri-fold mirrors once again, then leaned against the wall in defeat. "What's wrong with me, Grandma? Why can't I find anything that's just right for me? Am I really that difficult?" She slumped down into a nearby chair.

"You're just looking for the perfect fit, and that's not easy to find."

"I suppose," she said. "But nothing's going to be perfect, right? I mean, truly perfect." She sought out her grandmother's expression for an answer.

"You can force something to fit, but that doesn't make it right. Living with something that's uncomfortable or 'not quite right' is never a good thing."

Jessica tried to swallow the lump in her throat before responding. "What are you saying?"

Her grandmother's eyes watered a bit. "I'm just saying—if you could have anything you wanted, absolutely anything, what would it be?"

"Are we talking dresses here, or something else?"

"You tell me." The older woman suddenly took on a determined, maternal look. "Tell me about your dream wedding, Jessica."

"My dream wedding?"

"Yes. If you could have anything you wanted, what would you have?" The silver-haired beauty eased her way into a chair.

Jessica pursed her lips as she thought of her answer. "Well, the wedding of my dreams, the one I've always hoped for, would be very romantic but also a little theatrical, which I know Nathan would absolutely hate. There would be a stringed quartet playing in the background and candles all over the place. I know a church wedding would be nice—traditional—but I really see a more surreal setting, more like a, a. . ." She knew what she wanted to say, but didn't dare.

"A theater?" Her grandmother finished for her.

Jessica shrugged. "Yes, or something like that. Anyway, the music would be the foundation for the whole event, and all of the love songs would definitely be sung in Italian. There would be a backdrop—like a set, with painted scenes from Italy. Maybe some Roman columns—to add a little romance—with swags of sheer fabric draped between them and some twinkling lights reflecting through."

"Sounds beautiful."

"And," Jessica continued, more excited now, "if I had my way, I wouldn't even wear a traditional wedding dress at all. I'd pick something with a long, flowing skirt. Chiffon, maybe. Lots of flow. Loose, romantic sleeves. Something very dramatic."

"More like a costume from one of your operas?"

"Yes, actually." Jessica felt a sense of relief as the words were spoken. "And not necessarily white," she continued, "which I know would probably upset everyone. But I just see this as a nontraditional sort of wedding—a staged event."

"Right, right."

"I'd like to see a little color, even in my gown. Muted, of course. If we're going with a Mediterranean theme."

"*Are* you going with a Mediterranean theme?"

"Well, I've tried to tell Nathan my ideas, but he's got a more traditional approach in mind. Not that he's being stubborn. He's not." Jessica drew in a deep breath. "He's almost too nice about it all, but I can see it in his eyes. He's very 'in the box'—which is fine. That's just who he is, and I appreciate that about him. He's solid, stable."

"Romantic?"

"Well, I can't expect everything from one person," Jessica said slowly. "But I'm fine with that. I really am."

"Humph."

"Besides," Jessica said, trying to turn the conversation in another direction, "I don't want to hurt him by insisting on having my own way. That would be wrong. And I'm more than willing to compromise."

"Your wedding plans, you mean?" Another penetrating gaze.

"Of course. What else would I be compromising?"

Her grandmother's wrinkled brow alarmed her. "You're a wise girl, Jess. And I know you'll make the right decision."

"About the dress or the Mediterranean theme?"

"About everything. Your happiness is my first concern." Her precious grandmother suddenly grew more serious. "I'm sorry I said that, honey. Truth be told, finding God's perfect will in all of this is my first concern. After that, your happiness is right up there. I want you to be so blissfully in love that you can't see straight."

Jessica smiled. "Thanks."

"But," her grandmother continued, "I also want to see you fulfill your dreams in other areas of your life. Your father worked hard so that you could have music lessons as a child. I don't ever want you to forget the musical gift he saw in you from the time you were young. It's still there, you know."

Jessica felt tears begin to well up in her eyes and pushed them away with the back of her fist. "I know that."

"Just don't forget it, that's all I'm saying. It's one thing to be happy in love, another to be happy in life. A healthy bride needs both."

"Aren't they one and the same?" Jessica tried to force the lump down her throat, but it refused to budge.

Her grandmother shrugged. "Sometimes it seems that way, but answering the individual call of God in your life is critical. Before those vows are taken, I mean. So many people try to do it the other way around. They marry without ever discovering who they are, first."

"I. . ." Jessica couldn't seem to finish the sentence.

"When your grandfather passed away, I thought my life had ended," the silver-haired woman continued. "At first I was terrified. But those years alone gave me a chance to rediscover who I was, the things I had hoped and dreamed for as a young girl. By the time I met Buck, I was more sure of myself than I had been for years. When I married him, he knew he was getting a bride with some self-confidence."

"You're a strong woman. I know that. And I am, too."

"Jessica." Her grandmother stood and placed her hands on Jessica's shoulders. "Turn and look close." Together, they turned to face the tri-fold mirror. What Jessica saw staring back at her was a downcast bride-to-be in a wedding dress that didn't quite fit. "There's so much inside of you waiting to be discovered, and I'm not trying to discourage you. I'm really not. Just set out on that journey, and God will show you what's around the bend. In your gifts, in your occupation, and in your relationship with Nathan."

Jessica reached up and embraced her grandmother, not even trying to stop the tears. "I know you're right."

"You're going to be a beautiful bride, honey, and that radiance is going to shine through like a light that can't wait to escape the darkness, because it will spring up from your innermost being. In the meantime, promise me you'll take the time for a little self-discovery."

Jessica nodded, and as she turned toward the dressing room, tears tumbled freely down her cheeks. She carefully slipped out of the wedding dress, contemplating all her grandmother had said. *It's one thing to be happy in love, another to be happy in life.* Had she really heard correctly?

Lord, I don't want to be selfish with these wedding plans. Help me to find my happiness in You, and not in others.

Or my music.

Jessica dejectedly pulled on her jeans and T-shirt. As she exited the dressing room, she turned to look in the mirror once again. A somber face greeted her. She forced a smile. *I'll work harder at being happy,* she assured herself. *Even if it means putting my dreams on hold awhile longer.*

With a renewed vigor in her step, she turned to face the challenges of the day.

๛

Mom, I appreciate your efforts, but—" Colin never had a chance to finish the sentence before his mother cut him off.

"Colin, you're avoiding the subject."

He quickly shifted the cell phone to the opposite shoulder. For thirty minutes she had been sharing her concerns about his lack of a personal life, and the phone had grown warm to the touch. It was actually beginning to bother his ear a little. With both hands on the steering wheel, there was little he could do about that. He guided the car north on Houston's busy Interstate 45 as she spoke.

"You're twenty-eight years old, Colin." She never missed a beat. "It's time you settled down. Found yourself a wife. Had a few kids. I mean, the opera is a good thing, but there's certainly more to life than music. It's one thing to follow your dreams; it's another to give up your personal life."

"I know, Mom." He turned on his signal to change lanes, nearly dropping the phone in the process.

"It's not like you haven't had plenty of opportunity. I don't know how you could resist all of those beautiful young women in the company. There have been dozens I would have picked out for you. Dozens."

Colin groaned inwardly. To be honest, none of the women who currently sang with the Dallas Metropolitan Opera suited him at all. Many were prima donnas, and the few who weren't already happened to be involved in relationships. Besides, the Lord had someone unique in mind for him. Someone who had given her heart to the Lord and shared his passion for the lost. Someone who recognized that any gifts she had were given by God and not something to be flaunted or admired.

In short, the woman he was waiting for might be a long time in coming. But Colin didn't mind the wait. Sure, he had grown a little lonely at times, but the busyness of his schedule helped. And once he returned to Dallas and the children's chorus kicked off, his free time would be zapped with a host of additional activities.

"Are you still with me?"

His mother's words brought him back to his senses, and he quickly responded in his most reassuring voice. "I'm here."

"I don't want you to think I'm lecturing, honey," she continued. "I know this is your own business. It's just that sometimes I wonder if I'll ever have grandchildren."

Colin smiled. Many times, he had thought of what his future would be like. A houseful of kids would be sheer bliss. He couldn't wait. But what choice did he have, really? "You'll have grandchildren, Mom," he assured her. "I'm looking forward to being a father someday."

"You'll be a great one." Her voice lifted. "And they'll be beautiful if they take after you."

"Mom."

"Just hear me out on this, Colin," she urged him. "Your career is very important to you. I know that. And I know you've been given a serious, God-given gift that few can comprehend or appreciate. But that gift, no matter how fully developed, will never be able to replace relationships. You need a healthy balance of both."

"I know." He sighed. "But, Mom—"

"Colin, I hate to do this," she said abruptly, "but there's someone calling on the other line. I've been waiting on a call from the cable company, so I'd better get it."

"I love you, Mom."

"I love you, too." With a click, she hung up.

For the next few moments Colin fought to focus on the road. His mother's words carried a sting. Many times he had wondered if he would ever marry, even wondered if perhaps God might require him to remain single so that he could accomplish more for the sake of the gospel.

But his heart told him otherwise. Truthfully, he longed for someone to love, someone to share his heart, his home, his life. . .his passion for music.

Lord, I know I might not find everything I'm looking for in one woman. If she's out there, Father, then please bring her to me. I don't want to miss Your plans for my life. I want someone to love. I want the joy—the happiness—that a relationship would bring.

In the meantime, Colin surmised, life at the opera would have to do.

six

Jessica clutched Nathan's hand as they moved through the crowd of people at Houston's annual Grand Opera Benefit Gala. She looked out across the beautiful foyer of the Wortham Theater, her hands tightly clutched to her chest. "I almost sang here."

"What, honey?" Nathan raised his voice to be heard above the din.

"Oh, nothing. I was just thinking out loud." Jessica paused as she looked around the room teeming with people. "I do love this place. Don't you?"

"It's okay." He shrugged.

"Just okay?" She looked around at the beautiful room with its exquisite décor and was reminded immediately of the day she had raced so quickly across this lobby, barely noticing its beauty.

"At least tonight won't be a total waste."

"What do you mean?"

"I'm taking mental notes. Looking at that buffet table is giving me ideas for our wedding reception." He pointed to their right.

"Really? Me, too." A beautiful array of foods was spread out before the opera patrons, beckoning, tempting. Smoked salmon, luscious fruit platters, finger sandwiches shaped into musical notes. It was all too amazing to take in. "So what were you thinking?"

"Basically, that all of this is just too frilly, you know what I mean? We should do more basic foods. None of this buffet line stuff. We need a sit-down dinner with good, solid food. Guy food."

Jessica's heart lurched. She had always envisioned a beautiful reception with a wonderful array of foods. Not expensive, of course. But everything would look and taste expensive. And the guests would be overwhelmed at the artistic beauty of it all. Grapes and strawberries would dangle over the edges of crystal bowls and a luscious fruit dip would sit nearby. Vegetable trays would be adorned with carrots cut to look like flowers, and broccoli sculpted to look like actual trees. She had a plan—an elegant, creative plan.

"All this talk about food is making me hungry." Nathan turned toward the buffet line. "What about you?"

"Nope. Not yet," she said. "Besides, I need to find Professor Wallace and see if he needs me. I'm supposed to be here to help." Tonight's event would benefit the Houston Grand Opera in a number of ways. Despite their recent rejection, Jessica still felt compelled to support the organization in any way she could. Besides, her favorite professor from the University of Houston had called specifically to ask for her assistance. She was to meet him at the school's booth on the northeast side of the room. If only she could find it.

"Go on." Nathan turned toward the food line. "I'll catch up with you later."

Jessica fought her way through the crowd, looking for the Moores School of Music booth. She located it—off in the distance, to her left—though she could barely make out Professor Wallace through the crowd. She quickly made her way in his direction, hardly able to squeeze through the throng of people. "Excuse me." She apologized as she accidentally bumped into a tall gentleman who blocked her way.

"No problem."

Jessica looked up in surprise as she heard the familiar voice. Colin Phillips stood directly in front of her. "Mr. Phillips."

His face lit up immediately. "Jessica." He extended his hand. "I wondered if I would see you here tonight. I take it you're an opera supporter as well as an amazing vocalist."

She felt her cheeks warm with embarrassment. "Yes, my music professor," she said, gesturing across the room, "got me involved during my junior year. I've seen every opera for the past three seasons. That's why I was so excited to finally get the chance to audition." Her voice faltered slightly. "But anyway, I'm really late."

"I'll walk with you, if you don't mind."

"Of course not."

She turned and began to make her way through the crowd with Mr. Phillips on her heels. Why her heart fluttered, she had absolutely no idea.

❧

Colin followed along behind Jessica Chapman as she made her way through the boisterous crowd. In her soft blue evening gown, with her auburn hair swept up like that, she wasn't difficult to keep track of. He envisioned her standing on a stage, singing in that beautiful blue dress.

All the way across the room, he fought the urge to ask her, one last time, to reconsider his offer to come to Dallas. *No. I won't do it.*

When they arrived at the university's booth, Colin had to smile. Jessica's professor, a short, bald gentleman, looked a little frazzled as he crawled up from under the table, where he had obviously been searching for something.

"Jessica!" The older man's face lit immediately. "I'm so glad you're here. I'm at my wit's end. I can't seem to find our brochures. And I need someone to visit with all of the potential students who stop by."

"Of course. I'd be happy to."

"I started a list for people to sign." He gestured toward a clipboard at the far end of the table, then immediately went to his knees again, resuming his search through a large cardboard box.

Colin smiled, in spite of himself. This fellow was quite a character.

Jessica went to retrieve the list, then began to chat with a young woman about music scholarships. Colin marveled at how easily she talked to strangers and how comfortable she seemed to be. *She has such an easy way about her.*

Professor Wallace stood, proudly waving a stack of brochures in his hand. "Found them!" He placed them on the table, then gave Colin a curious look.

Colin suddenly came to his senses. "I should introduce myself. I'm—"

"Jessica's fiancé, of course!" the older man added with a smile. He grabbed Colin's hand. "It's great to finally meet you."

"Actually, sir—"

"I've heard so much about you," the professor continued excitedly. "You've got quite a girl, let me tell you. She's got a voice like an angel, that one."

"Oh, don't I know it." Colin nodded emphatically. "Never heard anything like it, and I hear a lot of great voices."

"It's Nathan, right?" The professor began to spread the brochures out across the table.

"Well, actually, I'm—"

"I hate to brag, but I consider your fiancée to be my prodigy," Professor Wallace interrupted. "When she transferred to the university her sophomore year, I discovered her. She was in my choir at the time. But once I heard her sing solo. . ."

Jessica approached in the middle of his sentence. She gave the professor a look of curiosity.

"I know what you mean," Colin said excitedly. "The first time I heard Jessica sing, I just couldn't believe it. She reminded me of Beverly Sills. At a young age, of course."

"I agree completely!" The professor waved his arms dramatically. "Same quality. Same tone. And talk about a range."

"She's better than most of the professionals I've heard,"

Colin added. "And I've heard quite a few."

Jessica looked up at him, clearly stunned. "Beverly Sills? Better than most? Those might be slight exaggerations, gentlemen."

"You're one lucky man, Nathan." The older man extended his hand.

Colin caught Jessica's shocked expression. "Actually, sir, I—"

"But with your obvious love for music, I'd have to say that Jessica hasn't fared too poorly herself," the professor interrupted. "You know, it's not always easy to find someone who understands a vocalist's world. In fact, many of the mismatched musical relationships I've witnessed have ended on a sour note, if you know what I mean." He chuckled.

Jessica turned pale. "Professor Wallace, this isn't Nathan. This is—"

"The luckiest man on earth, if you ask me," the older man interrupted. "But, regardless of your name, young man, you'd better be prepared to hang on for dear life if you're marrying this girl. She's going places. And fast. She's already auditioned for the opera; did you know?"

"Yes, sir. Actually, I was there," Colin explained.

"Then you know what a jewel she is. And if I haven't said it already, you're one lucky guy." At that, the professor turned to speak to someone else.

Jessica grabbed Colin's arm. "Did you tell him you were my fiancé?"

"No."

"Where did he get that idea?"

Colin shrugged. "I have no idea."

"This is so embarrassing." She buried her face in her hands.

Colin reached out and gently pulled her hands down so he could see her eyes as he spoke. "It might be embarrassing," he said. "But it's also been enlightening. He was right about your voice, Jessica. He only confirmed what I already knew to be true. You are going places."

Her eyes filled with tears, and he let go of her hands so she could dab at them. "Do you mean that?"

"Of course." Colin gestured toward the professor. "He knows it, and I know it, too. But what about you? Do you know it? Have you made a decision about what you're going to do with this gift you've been given?"

Jessica sighed. "It is a gift," she acknowledged. "But I don't know what I ever did to deserve it."

"When God gives a gift, He doesn't attach any strings," Colin said. "We don't have to qualify for it. And I have it on good authority that the Lord is a lot easier on us than that audition panel you faced."

"No kidding." She chuckled.

"He invented music, you know. And I happen to believe He loves it."

"He does." A smile suddenly lit her face. "And I love it, too. I love the stories in the songs. I love the sound of the instruments warming up. I love the way it feels when the overture begins and the music swells. The whole auditorium just seems to come alive with an electricity that I can't explain." She closed her eyes, as if off in her own world. "And I know I'd love to have the privilege of actually standing up on the stage instead of just sitting in the audience." Her eyes flew open. "I'll get there someday."

"Someday." He dared not say another word.

Jessica's brow wrinkled. "In the meantime, I'm content to go on working to help others reach their dreams." She pointed to a young woman at the end of the table. "I just met that girl down there. Valerie. She's been interning with the junior division of the Houston Grand Opera, and she's considering the University of Houston for her education. I think I helped her make that decision just now."

"That's great, Jessica." *If only you could see how good you'd be at helping lots of young people like her. In Dallas.*

Jessica's fiancé appeared at her side with a plateful of food in his hand. He poked at it with a plastic fork. "How are you supposed to know what any of this stuff is, anyway? None of it looks edible."

"Nathan." She placed her hand on his arm.

"Hmm?" He seemed too preoccupied with his plate to pay much attention.

"Nathan," Jessica continued, "you remember Mr. Phillips."

Nathan looked up immediately, and, as their eyes met, Colin detected a look of animosity.

"Oh yeah. The music guy. From Dallas."

Colin extended his hand. "Please. Call me Colin."

Nathan shifted the plate and briefly shook hands. Very briefly. "So what were you two discussing?" he asked.

"Actually, I was visiting with Jessica's professor," Colin explained. "We were talking music."

"I don't know how anyone could handle all of this opera mumbo jumbo," Nathan said. He pressed a piece of salmon into his mouth and then continued. "But most of these people seem to be cut from the same mold."

"Nathan's not terribly musical," Jessica explained as she slipped her arm around his waist. "But he's learning."

Colin nodded in understanding.

Nathan shrugged. "I'm more at home with numbers. But that's what makes us so perfect for each other." He pulled Jessica close with his free arm, clearly conveying his message. "You know what they say about opposites attracting." He planted a kiss on her cheek.

"Yes, well," Colin said, "if you'll excuse me, I should probably head over to the other side of the room to meet up with the rest of my party. We've got some fund-raising ideas to talk over before I leave for Dallas."

"Are you going back tonight?" Jessica asked.

"In the morning, actually." Colin extended his hand in her direction. "It was nice to run into you once again, Miss Chapman. Maybe I'll have the opportunity to hear you sing again one day."

"Maybe." She gripped his hand a little longer than he had anticipated, and unspoken words traveled between them. When she withdrew it, her gaze shifted to the floor.

Colin nodded and smiled in her direction, then turned to leave. He couldn't help thinking of all Jessica would be missing, though he did not feel at peace about pursuing the discussion. The Lord clearly had someone else in mind.

The words "You're one lucky man!" rang out across the cacophony of sounds in the room. Colin turned to see the professor waving. He returned the gesture then headed in the opposite direction.

seven

Jess made her way up the aisle to the front of the church. Though the Sunday morning service had ended nearly half an hour ago, she felt compelled to linger a bit. Explaining this to Nathan had taken some doing, but she just couldn't leave the sanctuary. Not yet. Several issues weighed heavily on her heart, and she must find some answers. As a believer, she knew exactly where those answers would come from.

As she approached the altar area, Jessica felt the urge to drop to her knees. Perhaps the weight of life's decisions drove her down. Whatever the reason, she had to get alone with God—had to get His perspective on the issues at hand. As she knelt in prayer, Jessica poured her heart out. All of the things she had struggled with over the past few weeks now drove her to speak. Finally. God could be trusted with her thoughts, her emotions. He had created them, after all. The words seemed to tumble forth like autumn leaves on a crisp evening breeze.

"Lord, I know You love me. I feel Your love, Father. And I know You have a plan for my life. I don't want to make a mistake or waste time doing the wrong thing. I want to go where You want me to go and do what You want me to do. Anything else would be wrong. I'm tired of walking in my own strength, Lord. I'm tired of trying to make everyone happy and even more tired of pretending to be happy myself. What I need to know is what will make You happy. I want to please You, Father. I really do."

Then the tears started.

After a few moments of weeping in silence, Jessica drew in a deep breath. From out of nowhere, she suddenly felt compelled to sing. A worship song poured forth from her heart and lips. It reverberated across the room and seemed to take her to new heights, freeing her from the turmoil inside. As she sang her self-composed hymn of praise, courage arose inside, which prompted her to stand. She continued to sing as she made her way to the platform area of the church. From here, she could see the entire room. Though empty, she imagined it full of people and sang her heart out.

When the melody ended, she trembled uncontrollably. *What are You doing in me, Lord? Where did that song come from?* Had she composed it herself, or did it come from the very throne of God? On wobbly legs, she made her way down the steps and began to walk to the back of the sanctuary. She knew that something extraordinary had taken place. Something was stirring. Something big.

Daughter.

Jessica stopped in her tracks and listened intently for the Lord's unspoken words.

Daughter, I love you. You may not see, but I have awesome plans for you—plans for a hope and a future. Don't be afraid of what you can't see. I can see clearly enough for both of us.

Jessica wept until her chest ached. *Lord, I trust You.* The song of praise came to her lips again, and she sang as if kneeling at the throne of God. All the way out of the building, she sang. In the car, she sang. All the way home, she sang.

By the time she pulled the car into the driveway, Jessica knew what had to be done. She felt an inner peace she had never known before. Surprising words tripped across her tongue, and yet they felt just right. "I'm going to Dallas," she whispered with a smile.

Now came the hard part. She must tell the others. They were inside, probably already seated at the dinner table. She would tell them all at one time. The task would be easier that way. Jessica made her way through the front door and into the dining room, where they all looked up at her with expressions of curiosity.

"You okay?" Nathan asked as she seated herself.

"Great." She smiled warmly.

"We saved you a piece of chicken." Her mother gestured toward the platter on the table. One lone piece sat waiting. Jessica reached for it then loaded her plate with mashed potatoes, gravy, green beans, and a biscuit. Everyone went back to his or her prior conversations. No one seemed to notice her nervous condition except her grandmother and Grandpa Buck, who gazed at her with a knowing look from the opposite end of the table.

After a few bites, Jessica tapped the edge of her water glass with her spoon. When no one noticed, she cleared her throat—loudly. All faces turned her direction. "I have an announcement to make." The words trembled across her lips. All of the courage she had felt in the car seemed to have vanished.

Don't be afraid, Jessica.

"What is it, honey?" Her mother reached over and patted her hand. "You and Nathan aren't moving up the date, are you?"

Nathan stopped chewing long enough to answer. "Definitely not."

"No, that's not it. I have something else to announce."

"What's up, Jess?" Nathan used his napkin to wipe a bit of gravy from his mouth.

She swallowed hard before speaking. "I've decided to accept Mr. Phillips's offer and move to Dallas for the next six months. I'm going to take the internship—if it's not too late."

Chaos immediately erupted as they talked over one another. Jessica couldn't make much sense out of any of it until Nathan's voice rose above the rest. "You're doing what?" he asked.

"I'm going to Dallas."

"Jess, are you sure about this?" Her mother twisted a cloth napkin into knots.

"Yes, I am." She placed her fork down on the table and prepared herself for a lengthy conversation on the matter.

Kent reached across the table and grabbed the potatoes. "Big mistake, Sis. Long-distance relationships never work out."

"We can make this work." She sought out Nathan's gaze. He didn't look terribly convinced. "I know that God has big plans for my life."

"Marrying me is that big plan." Nathan's words seemed to rock the table.

"Part of it," she said softly. "But there's more to me than just being someone's bride."

From across the table, Jessica saw her grandmother's nod of assurance and forged ahead. "If I don't take the time to find out who I am—and what God's call on my life is—then I won't be a good wife. I won't be a good mother. I might not even be a good person. It's critical for me to discover God's will for me, personally."

"What are you saying?" Nathan's brow wrinkled.

"I'm not putting a stop to the wedding plans, if that's what you're worried about. I'll be coming back and forth nearly every weekend. At least every other. It's just a four-hour drive, after all. And we have the Internet. We can stay connected online every day with instant messages and e-mail. This doesn't have to be complicated."

"You've just got so much going on already, Jess," her mother said. "I hope you can handle it all. Once you get up there, your workload will be really heavy."

"I know, and I'm looking forward to that. It's not like I haven't thought all of this through. I have. Carefully. I've prayed about it. I've weighed my options. And I know this is right. I just hope you can all trust my judgment to make this decision."

The room grew silent, and Jessica felt like a criminal at an inquisition. *Lord, is this what it feels like to be alone in your principles?*

Her grandmother grinned mischievously then tapped her own water glass. "I have a few comments to make on the matter," she said. Everyone turned their attention in her direction. "I, for one, trust my granddaughter." The older woman spoke slowly, deliberately. "She's proven herself to be reliable over the years, and I have no cause to doubt her judgment now. If Jessica feels the Lord is leading her to Dallas, so be it. Whether right or wrong, she will discover His plan in the process. I think we should let her be the grown-up woman that she is, and that's all I have to say on the matter." She leaned back in her seat and folded her arms.

Once again, the room erupted in lively conversation. Jessica let her weight rest against the back of the chair and turned her head from side to side as comments flowed freely. Only when she looked to the opposite end of the table, into her grandmother's adoring eyes, did she feel the strength of agreement.

❧

"Mr. Phillips? Mr. Phillips!"

Colin brought the church choir to a halt as eighty-two-year-old Walter Malone fought to get his attention. "What's up, Walter?"

"Your cell phone is going off. Even with my bad ears, I can hear it." The older man pointed to his hearing aid and grinned.

Colin heard the ringing then but shrugged. "I can call them back—whoever it is. We're in the middle of practice right now, and with all the weeks I've missed, you guys are out of shape." The thirty-some-odd choir members of His Word Community Church began to grumble. Colin didn't mind. In fact, he had grown used to it. For three years now, he had served as volunteer choir director at this small community church on the north side of Dallas. Its members, most in their golden years, lived to torment him. He loved every minute with them.

"Never know—could be missing the most important call of your life!" Walter shook his head.

"Could be your future missus on the phone," seventy-four-year-old Ida Sullivan added. "But if you don't want to take the call, that's your choice. 'Course, it's about time you found yourself a girlfriend, if you want my opinion on the matter. Not that anybody ever listens to my opinion." She began to grumble under her breath.

Colin chuckled. "Okay, okay. I'll get it." He reached to pick up the phone but noticed he had already missed the call. He glanced curiously at the area code. *Someone from the Houston area. Lord, is it possible. . . ?*

Suddenly his heart began to race. "Why don't we take a break for about five minutes, and then we'll go over that last section again." He bounded from the stage and made his way to the back of the auditorium as he redialed the number. It rang once, twice, three times, then a familiar voice greeted him.

"Hello?"

"Jessica, is that you?" Colin felt his spirits lift immediately.

"It's me." She sounded more cheerful than before. He liked that sound.

"It's good to hear from you." He continued to walk, though Walter now joined him. Ida stood nearby, clearly straining to hear.

"Do you have a minute?" Jessica asked.

"I do." He tried to signal Walter away with his eyes, but the older man simply wasn't taking the hint.

"I have something to tell you," Jessica said. "Something I hope will be good news."

His heart pounded double time. *Lord, are You really this good to me? Have You answered my prayer for a director of the children's chorus?* "I could use some good news," he responded.

"I just wanted to let you know—I mean, if the offer still holds—that I'd like to come."

"Really? You're coming to Dallas?" He let out a whoop that nearly sent poor Walter reeling. "Jessica, that's great. What did your family say? What about your fiancé? Is he okay with this?" Immediately Colin regretted asking. These were personal questions and really none of his business. Besides, at the word *fiancé*, Ida waved her arms in defeat and turned to walk the other way.

"They'll get used to the idea," Jessica said. "But I have to follow the Lord's leading."

"And He's leading you here. Are you sure?" *Lord, I want her to be very, very sure. I don't want to take her away from anything You've planned for her there.*

"I'm sure," she said. "I'll be traveling back and forth on weekends as I'm able. I know I can make this work. And, to be honest, I can't wait to meet the kids and get to work. Which reminds me, when should I come? Also, do you have any ideas about housing? And what sort of vocal materials should I bring with me for warm-ups and practices? I've got some great children's pieces."

"We really need to talk more about this," Colin agreed. "There will be quite a few details to iron out. But the Dallas Met is prepared to offer you a place to stay—all expenses paid, plus a modest salary. And, as I said before, a place in the chorus of our upcoming shows." At that, Walter elbowed him in the ribs. "Uh, could I call you later tonight? I'm, uh. . ." Colin whispered into the receiver. He looked into Walter's imploring eyes. "I'm in the middle of something right now."

"Oh, sure. I'm leaving for our evening service at church in about an hour, but I'll be back around nine. Is that too late?"

"Nope. Should work out just right."

"Well, thank you for calling me back," she said. "I feel a lot better now that the decision is made. You know how that goes."

"Yes, I do. And thank you for taking the time to reconsider," he added. "I'm so anxious to see what the Lord is going to do."

"Me, too. Well, I guess I'll let you get back to work now. Have a great evening."

"You, too, Jessica." He hung the phone up and turned to face thirty pairs of inquisitive eyes.

" 'You, too, Jessica,' " Walter spoke in a lovey-dovey voice.

"Now, Walter. It's not like that."

"I'd say. Especially if she's already got a beau," Ida threw in. " 'Course, I haven't met him yet. Don't rightly know if he's the right man for her, but that's for the Lord to determine, not me. Not that anyone ever listens to my opinions anyhow." She began to mutter again, and Colin turned his attention to getting the choir back in place on the stage.

Somehow, though, he couldn't keep his thoughts or the tempo of the music straight. Everything seemed to have suddenly, ridiculously gone askew.

eight

Colin spent the last Saturday in September thumbing through a stack of children's résumés. He stifled a yawn as he read over them for the umpteenth time. He tried not to let his exhaustion stop him from the task at hand, though he had slept precious few hours over the past week. Thankfully, auditions for the adult performance of *Madame Butterfly* had gone well. With a full cast firmly established, rehearsals would soon be under way.

However, narrowing the list for the children's production of *Amahl and the Night Visitors* might prove to be a bit more difficult. Fifty talented children would be auditioning tomorrow afternoon. Colin held their résumés in his hand. Out of that group, he could choose only twenty. How would he ever decide who to keep and who to cut? Which hearts would be encouraged, and which ones broken?

Thankfully, he wouldn't have to make those decisions alone. Colin would have Jessica Chapman's help. He glanced at his watch. She should be arriving—actually, she should be pulling into the Dallas area right about now, if everything went according to plan. He'd give her the day to settle in, then call her first thing in the morning, perhaps even invite her to church. Then, armed and ready, they would dive right into the auditions.

Colin leaned back in his chair, and relief washed over him. For years, he had dreamed of starting a children's company in the Dallas area. God had answered his prayers just a few short months ago when the board of the Metropolitan Opera agreed to finance his dream. He had been given free rein to oversee the project, but with so much on his plate already, selecting a vocal director had been critical to his own survival.

His mind drifted to Jessica once again. Colin had thanked the Lord daily for providing just the right person for the job. And what a job it would be. With fifty children slotted for auditions, he could easily predict a couple of sleepless nights ahead. His eyes grew heavy as he glanced through the children's résumés one last time. *Lord, help us make the right decisions. I want to give opportunity to the ones You've chosen. Help us, Father.*

❧

Jessica chatted with her mom by cell phone as they caravanned into the Dallas area. "Are you getting sleepy?" she asked as she caught a glimpse of her mother's car in the rearview mirror.

"Not too bad," her mother said with a yawn. "What about you?"

"I'm wide awake." Jessica fought to balance the cell phone against her ear as she glanced over at Nathan. He sat snoring in the seat next to her. "Nathan's passed out, but that's a good thing. He has an exam Monday morning, and he needs all the rest he can get. I didn't mind driving, anyway," she added. "I need to get used to it." She glanced over at him, nearly dropping the phone in the process. It warmed her heart to see him sleeping so peacefully after his rough week. He had been so good to give up his Saturday to help her move, especially in light of his objections.

"I suppose." Her mother sighed. "How much farther?"

"Mmm." Jessica glanced down at the printed e-mail. "Looks like we're only about twenty minutes from the exit. How are you guys doing back there?" She peered into the rearview mirror once again.

"We're fine, honey. Your brother is preoccupied with his new pocket organizer, and Andrew's reading a history book."

"Figures. What about you? How are you holding out?"

"I'm a little stiff from driving so long. I'll be glad to get there."

"Me, too." Jessica stretched. "But it's good to talk to you. Again. What did we ever do before cell phones?"

"I can't remember. But speaking of phones, I should probably hang up now. I need to save all the minutes I can. With you living in Dallas now. . ." Her mother's voice seemed to break.

"It's going to be okay, Mom," Jessica said. "You'll hardly have time to miss me before I'm home again. Wait and see."

"Okay, honey. Guess I'll talk to you when we get there."

"I love you."

"I love you, too."

As she ended the call, Jessica leaned back against the seat and yawned. She glanced at the clock. *Only four sixteen? It feels more like midnight.* Then again, her day had started pretty early. Loading the car had taken awhile. Though a furnished apartment awaited her in Dallas, Jessica still had to pack her clothes, music, and personal items. As for kitchenware, her mother had pressed enough of that into her trunk to last Jess a lifetime.

Not that she planned to spend a lifetime away from home. The next six months would fly by. She felt sure of it. With September drawing to a close, Jessica had just a few precious weeks of fall left to prepare a team of youngsters to perform in their first Christmas opera—after tomorrow's auditions, anyway. And what fun she would have getting them ready!

Jessica's mind wandered. Her distraction nearly caused her to miss the appropriate exit. Thankfully, she looked up just in time. With a nervous glance in the rearview mirror, she discovered her mother had made the exit, as well.

Within minutes, she pulled her car to the front of Northgate Crossing apartments. As she stopped and shifted into park, she glanced over at Nathan, who still snored loudly. *Let him sleep a few more minutes. He deserves it.* She climbed from the car and stretched before waving to her mother and stepfather. They gave the apartment complex an admiring look.

"Not bad," Andrew said.

"It is nice, isn't it?" Jessica felt a wave of contentment pass over her as she turned toward the office. "But I'd better get in there and pick up my key. I think they close at five. I'm cutting it pretty close."

Minutes later, she turned the shiny silver key to open the door of her very first apartment. Stepping inside, she gave a whistle. "Wow." She looked over the spacious living room, fully decked out with plush furniture and complementary décor.

"Looks like you won't be suffering much, Sis." Kent pushed past her with an armload of clothes. "Where do you want these, anyway?"

"In the bedroom." She led the way into the large front bedroom. It, too, took her by surprise. She could certainly learn to adapt to her new surroundings without much trouble.

"Not bad, not bad." Kent dropped the clothes on the bed, then headed out to the car for more. "If this is how opera singers live, I might want to take a few voice lessons myself."

"Very funny."

Nathan entered the room with a suitcase in hand. "Found a closet yet?" he asked.

"I'm guessing it's through that door." She pointed to her left. He stifled a yawn, then tossed the suitcase inside and turned back toward the front door.

Jessica gave the place a thorough looking over, more than pleased with her new home. *Thank You, Lord. You've been too good to me.* She could almost envision sharing this home, this beautiful home, with Nathan after their wedding. Almost. *Stop thinking like that. He would never agree to move to Dallas. This is just for a season, not a lifetime.*

"Knock, knock!" A chipper female voice brought Jessica back to reality. She turned to discover a young woman, blond and extremely tanned, standing in her open doorway. "Just wanted to stop by and say howdy," the petite beauty said with a smile. "I'm Kellie."

"I'm Jessica." She made her way to the door and extended her hand in greeting.

"I know." The girl's eyes twinkled merrily. "My sister has been talking about you for days."

"Your sister?"

"Katie. She sings with the Dallas Metropolitan Opera," Kellie explained. "We live right next door. She helped Colin find the apartment for you. Of course, she'd do anything for that guy. She's head over, if you know what I mean."

"Oh, I see. Well, thank her for me, okay?"

"I'm sure you two will be best buds." The blond sighed. "But me, well. . ." She laughed. "I'm completely tone-deaf. Don't care a thing about opera. Hope that doesn't offend you."

"Doesn't offend me." Nathan approached with another armload of clothes.

"Me, either," Jessica added. "Honestly."

"I can brew a mean cup of coffee, though." Kellie's lips curled up in a cute smile. "And I'm great if you ever want to chat about boyfriends or broken hearts or stuff like that."

"Thanks." Jessica glanced up at Nathan, whose eyes seemed fixed on the blond bombshell. "Um, speaking of boyfriends. This is my fiancé, Nathan."

Nathan nearly dropped the armload of clothes as he extended his hand. Kellie shook it vigorously.

"Nice to meet you," the perky young blond said.

"You, too." Nathan glanced at the ground and withdrew his hand.

"So," she said, "is there anything I can do to help?"

At that moment, Kent passed through the open doorway

with a box of pots and pans. He nearly tripped over his own feet as his gaze fell on Kellie. "Uh, Jess?"

"Yeah?"

"Could I, uh, talk to you in the bedroom?"

She trudged along behind him, leaving Nathan alone in the doorway with the blond.

"Who is that?" her brother asked, barely above a squeak.

Jessica shrugged. "She's just a neighbor who stopped by to say hello. Why?"

"Introduce me."

"Get a grip, Kent."

"No, I mean it." He spoke insistently. "Introduce me. But make me look good. Say something great about me."

With a groan, Jessica made her way to the doorway once again, this time taking pains to carefully introduce her brother to Kellie. When the vivacious young woman offered to give the newcomers a tour of the complex, Jessica declined, but Kent followed behind the boisterous blond like an obedient puppy. *Great. Now I've lost him completely.*

Jessica continued to unload the car with some assistance from her mother and Nathan, while Andrew drove off in search of a restaurant for dinner. She could hardly keep her thoughts straight. When they finished, she plopped down onto the sofa, completely exhausted. *If I sit here much longer, I'll fall asleep.*

Her mother joined her, letting out a groan as she sat. "I'm getting too old for this."

"Mom!" Jessica shook her head in disbelief. "You're not old."

"I haven't helped anyone move in years. It's a lot of work."

"No kidding." Nathan dropped into a wingback chair across from the sofa. "And to think we have to move you back in six months. Then move again into our own place. That's a lot of moving in one year's time."

Jessica shrugged. "I'm sorry. I really am."

Andrew appeared in the doorway. "Anyone hungry?"

"Starved," Jessica and her mother said in unison.

"I found a great Mexican restaurant just a couple of blocks away," Andrew said. "Let's grab a bite together before we head back home."

"Good luck finding Kent." Jessica chuckled.

"Where is he?" Andrew glanced at his watch.

Nathan stood and stretched. "Who knows. But don't worry. I'll track him down. The sooner we get on the road, the better. I've got a lot of studying left to do before the weekend is over." He headed outside to look for Kent.

Jessica enjoyed a few moments of quiet conversation with her mother and Andrew until her brother burst through the door.

"I'm in love!" He clutched his heart and acted as if he would faint.

"Honestly, Kent." Jessica rolled her eyes. "Not again."

"This time it's the real thing. I think I'm moving to Dallas."

"Nothing impulsive about this boy." Andrew patted him on the back.

"Well, before you up and marry this girl, would you like to have some dinner?" his mother asked. "Mexican food."

"I guess." Kent sighed loud enough to alert the entire apartment building.

As they gathered up their belongings and headed to the door, Jessica realized Nathan still hadn't returned. "Anyone seen my fiancé?" she asked.

"Oh, he'll be here in a minute," Kent said. "He and Kellie are talking about the stock market. Turns out, she's a broker. Isn't that amazing? I mean, isn't she amazing?"

"Amazing." Jessica smiled at her brother's antics.

Nathan soon appeared at the door, and they headed out to the restaurant. Over a plateful of enchiladas, Jessica decided to share some things that had been weighing heavily on her heart. She chose her words carefully. "I don't want any of you to think I've lost interest in planning the wedding."

Nathan shrugged his response. "I'm not worried, babe."

"No need to be." She gave him a hug.

"We know you better than that, honey."

"I know there's still so much to think about," Jessica continued. "We'll need to settle on some invitations when I come home weekend after next."

"True." He scooped a chip full of salsa into his mouth. "Or," he said after swallowing, "I guess I could just leave that part up to you. I've got a lot on my plate between now and then. No pun intended." He gestured to his half-empty plate and grinned.

"You wouldn't mind?" She looked at him curiously.

"Nope. I'm so busy with school. Besides, anything you pick will be great. I trust your judgment."

"Really?" *That's odd.* Jessica tried not to read too much into his lack of enthusiasm.

Her mother reached out and grasped her hand. "I'll give you as much help as you need or want."

"Thanks, Mom."

"And I'm only a phone call away. Promise me you won't be a stranger, Jess." Her mom's eyes grew misty.

"Trust me. I won't. I'm going to miss all of you so much." Tears sprang to her eyes, and she brushed them away. "But I know that God has a plan for me, and I'm so excited about what He's doing. Thank you, all of you, for being so understanding."

Jessica's mother reached over and gave her a warm embrace. Andrew smiled his reassurance from across the table. Kent went on talking about Kellie, the love of his life.

And Nathan. . .

Nathan seemed to have drifted off to sleep, sitting straight up.

nine

The first two weeks in Dallas flew by. When the auditions for the much-anticipated children's production drew to a close, Jessica finally had a moment to catch her breath. The whole process had placed her squarely in the center of a musical whirlwind. She loved every whimsical moment and immediately grew to love the children selected for the prized roles, as well.

In her heart, Jessica knew she had been born for this very thing—to train and mentor young people in the classical vocal style. In the same way that her father had supported her musical gifts, she would encourage these budding stars. Already, Jessica could see that her input would have tremendous payoff, both vocally and psychologically. Nothing could make her feel better.

The knowledge that she would soon be singing alongside some of the best-trained voices in the country left her speechless. Jessica could hardly wait to join the chorus of *Madame Butterfly*. Her formal audition for the company would come in a couple of weeks, though her position in the chorus had already been secured by Colin, who—she had recently learned—would play one of the major roles in the production.

Her lips curled upward in an unexpected smile as she thought about Colin Phillips. More than a mentor and guide, he had already turned out to be a great friend. And his vocal ability left her speechless. When she heard him sing to the children for the first time, Jessica felt an unexplainable kinship with him. His rich baritone voice had reminded her of someone, something—though she couldn't put her finger on who or what.

Jessica truly came to know herself in Dallas. Somehow life just seemed more exciting here. The city itself seemed to be alive with electrical energy. In spite of a few moments of homesickness for Nathan and her family, Jessica never once regretted her decision to move to this thriving metropolis. Not that she had much time to ponder the matter. In no time at all, it seemed, she was on her way back to Houston for a weekend visit.

As she drove, Jessica spent a great deal of time in thought and in prayer. *Lord, You've been so good to me. I know I don't deserve all of this, but thank You. And thank You for trusting these children to my care. Help me to be a good example to them. I know it's not specifically a Christian environment, but help me to shine Your light in any way I can. And help me to balance my life in Dallas with my life at home. I pray Your perfect will is done in my life, Father. Amen.*

She continued south on Interstate 45, completely lost in her thoughts. On more than one occasion, Jessica challenged herself to think of other things besides the goings-on in Dallas. So much in her life had changed, and yet she must remain focused on the task at hand. Nathan would be waiting at home. Together, they would finalize their guest list, and then she would place an order for invitations. In all truthfulness, she had scarcely spent more than a moment or two thinking about the wedding, what with all of the events of the past few days, but this weekend at home would help.

Home.

Somehow traveling back to Houston put things in perspective. And seeing Nathan again would be great. She could hardly wait, in fact. There were so many stories to share—so much news to relay. He would be thrilled to hear it all.

Then again, he hadn't had much time to call or send e-mails over the past two weeks. Between his work schedule and college classes, he seemed to be almost as swamped as she. *Never mind that. We'll have the whole weekend together. It will be great.*

Jessica arrived home late that Friday night, breathlessly anticipating all that lay ahead. Her mother greeted her at the door with a kiss on each cheek and excited squeals. "I've missed you so much!"

Jessica felt tears in her eyes as she melted in her mother's arms. "I've missed you, too, Mom." It felt wonderful to be home once again, and she could hardly wait to catch up on all that had happened.

"Well, look who's here." Andrew appeared in the doorway. "The lost sheep returns home at last."

"I wasn't lost," Jessica said with a smile. *In fact,* she pondered, *I feel like I've finally found myself.*

"Well, come on in, stranger." Andrew grabbed her suitcase and ushered her into the living room.

Kent joined them, and everyone promptly began to ask question after question.

"What do you think about. . . ?"

"Have you had a chance to. . . ?"

"I can hardly wait to tell you. . . ."

On and on they went. After a few moments of talking over one another, the conversation finally fell into some semblance of order, and Jessica was able to share her heart. She told them about the children. She told them about the magnificent theater and its intricate design. She shared some funny stories of things her boisterous neighbors, Katie and Kellie, had done to welcome her to the neighborhood. In short, she finally had a chance to put a voice to all of the Lord's goodness in her life over the past two weeks.

Andrew and her mother laughed at each antic and added their own stories of all that had transpired since her absence. They had missed her terribly but had managed to take advantage of the spare bedroom by purchasing a new computer and desk to replace her missing furniture. Kent admitted, with reddened cheeks, that he had e-mailed Kellie on a number of occasions but had yet to hear back from her. He claimed her computer must be broken, though Jessica certainly knew better.

"Tell me about the church," she urged everyone. "How are the kids? How is Mrs. Witherspoon?"

"Oh, you've missed so much already!" Her mother lit up with excitement. "The children are going to be performing a Christmas musical. Something with an angel theme. Believe it or not, Mrs. Witherspoon has already held auditions. Rehearsals start next Sunday afternoon."

"You're kidding."

"No, I'm not."

Her mother laughed. "She's really in her element, but who would have guessed it?"

"No kidding." Jessica couldn't be more surprised. Funny, she also felt a tad bit of jealousy creep up at the news.

"She's always been such a 'behind-the-scenes' sort of gal—letting you take charge of everything," her mother continued. "But you should have heard her talking to Pastor Meeks about the set design and costumes. She's amazing."

"Wow. That's great." Though startled, Jessica breathed a huge sigh of relief, recognizing that this, another piece to the puzzle, had been orchestrated by the Lord.

They tumbled back into lively conversation, and time flew by. Jessica stayed up well past midnight, filling her family's ears with every wonderful detail of the past two weeks. When at last it came time to rest, she could hardly keep her eyes open. She fell asleep on the sofa, too tired to argue with the lumpy pillow or the itchy cushions. She awoke on Saturday morning with a stiff neck. However, her heart seemed to be dancing.

Jessica could hardly wait to see Nathan. After a brief phone call, they arranged to meet at a local pancake house for breakfast. He met her at the door of the restaurant thirty minutes later and swept her into his arms.

"How's my girl?" he asked as soon as their lips parted.

Her animated response seemed to flow like water. "I'm great! But I've missed you so much. How are you? How is school? How's work?"

"Whoa, whoa!" He put his hands up in protest. "Too many questions. Too fast."

"I'm sorry." She wrapped her arm around his waist, and they entered the restaurant together. "I just feel like we have so much to talk about and so little time."

"Yes, well. . ." He drew in a deep breath. "Less time than you know."

"What do you mean?"

"I have an appointment at noon," he explained. "Then I'm supposed to meet my study group at three."

"You're kidding."

"Wish I was. But let's not let that stop us from having a good time while we're together." He took hold of her hand.

"I just miss you." She pouted. *How could he schedule a study session on my weekend at home? Doesn't he know how much I need to be with him? And why did he have to have a meeting today, of all days?*

Nathan gave her a curious look just as the server appeared. "Well, I miss you, too, Jess." His voice dropped to a hoarse whisper. "But I'm not the one who moved away, remember? And I still have things to do, things that can't wait."

She followed in numb silence to a table at the rear of the room. Suddenly, everything she had wanted to say seemed to vanish from her mind. A distance seemed to have opened up between them. *What's happening here?*

Jessica immediately determined to narrow the gap as best she could. Instead of telling Nathan any of her stories, she listened attentively while he shared all that had happened at college over the past two weeks. She held her tongue when he told her of an idea his mother had given him regarding the wedding reception. She nodded in agreement when he talked about the upcoming honeymoon to Germany.

In short, she kept all of her excitement inside, in the hope that this feeling of sadness would disappear. And yet, as his conversation shifted to less appealing things—the stock market, his latest accounting classes, and the advantages of lower interest rates—all Jessica could think about were her own tales. She tried to push them down, but they would not go away.

By the end of the meal, Jessica felt as if she could hardly remain quiet any longer. She quickly shared a few details of the past two weeks, and Nathan listened intently. *He is interested.* He seemed especially curious to hear about her neighbors and their antics, asking on more than one occasion if Kellie had corresponded with Kent. By the end of the meal, Jessica felt safe and secure once again.

They parted with a quick embrace, and Nathan assured her of his love. *He just misses me. But everything will be all right as long as we get some time alone together.* She would make sure that happened. Somehow. In the meantime, she would stay focused. That would certainly help.

The rest of the day seemed to fly by. Jessica thumbed through dozens of invitation samples but couldn't seem to settle on anything she thought they would both like. Sunday morning arrived quicker than she could have imagined, and she attended church with her family. Then, before she even had time to think about it, Jessica found herself on the road once more. All the way back to Dallas, her mind reeled. She tried to concentrate on wedding plans but instead found her thoughts drifting to the opera, and especially to the children awaiting her at home.

Home. Hmm.

So many exciting adventures lay ahead, and she had a lot of plans to make. Thankfully, she wouldn't be alone in any of them.

Jessica smiled as she thought of Colin. What a wonderful, godly man he had turned out to be. His love for the opera was surpassed only by his love for the Lord. *And the children.* He seemed to be completely taken with each one. She fully understood and appreciated his dedication to them, especially the ones who came from underprivileged families in the inner city. Many would never have received an opportunity to be trained at no cost if he hadn't implemented this program.

Thank You, Lord, for giving Colin this idea. How wonderful for these children to get the chance to sing in front of a real audience. And thank You for letting me participate. I'm so excited, Father.

Jessica consumed herself with thoughts of the upcoming week. Though she already missed Nathan terribly, she would see him very soon. In fact, he would be flying up next Saturday afternoon to escort her to a lavish fund-raiser dinner for the new children's program. She could hardly wait. In the meantime, she still had rehearsals with the children and her audition for *Madame Butterfly.*

With so many thoughts tumbling madly, Jessica could barely keep her mind on the road. By the time she arrived back in Dallas late Sunday evening, she felt fully awake and alive with excitement. Tomorrow simply couldn't come soon enough.

❧

Colin checked the time on several occasions Sunday afternoon. He knew Jessica would be driving back today and prayed for her safety. As he headed off to church for choir practice, he planned the week ahead. There were so many details to attend to. *Thank You, Lord, for giving me someone to share that responsibility.* Somehow, just knowing Jessica would be back on the job tomorrow morning made everything fine again.

As he steered his car into the church parking lot Sunday evening, Colin's cell phone rang. He grabbed it, then glanced at the number. "Oh no. Not again." For weeks, he had been fending off calls from one of the young women in the company. Katie Conway. She had expressed more than a little interest in him. *I don't want to be rude to her, but. . .*

Would it be wrong to simply ignore the call?

On the fourth ring, he answered. *Might be something urgent.* After all, she was a key player in the upcoming opera and needed to be assured, even pacified a lot. He didn't really mind—for the sake of the show. "Hello?" He spoke hesitantly.

"Oh, Colin, I'm so glad you answered." Katie immediately dove into a lengthy discussion about a problem she appeared to be having with a particular vocal number in the opera. "Would you mind, I mean—you don't have to. . . But would you mind coming by my place later this evening?" she asked. "I'm having such a difficult time with this one section of music, and having you here to sing along with me would be so helpful."

Colin glanced at his watch and started to explain that he was running late for choir practice. Just then, he heard a tapping on his car window. He looked up to see Ida Sullivan, standing with her arms crossed.

"You're late." The older woman mouthed the words and pointed to her watch.

Colin shrugged and gestured toward the phone, trying all the while to think of an answer to Katie's suggestion. "I, uh. . . I'm in the middle of something right now," he spoke quietly into the phone. "Actually, I'm at church."

"Oh, I'm sorry." He thought he heard a little sniffle. "I shouldn't have bothered you. I know you're so busy."

"It's no bother," he assured her. Ida continued to tap at his window. "But I'm afraid I've already got plans tonight, so I won't be much help to you."

Katie sighed loudly. "That's okay. Jessica will be back in town in a while. I know she won't mind giving me a hand with the music. She's great on the keyboard, anyway, and she's such a good sport."

She'll be exhausted.

"I guess I'll see you tomorrow then." Katie's voice lifted slightly. "And thanks so much for being such a great friend, Colin."

"Good-bye, Katie." He hung up, feeling like a traitor. *Lord, I don't want to lead her on, but I don't know how to let her know I'm not interested without hurting her feelings.*

Just then, Ida knocked on his window again. Colin opened the car door and stepped outside.

"Talking to your girlfriend?" she asked.

"Nope. Just a business acquaintance." He began to walk toward the church. She trudged along behind him.

"How am I ever going to get you married off if you won't settle on a girl?"

"Ida, really."

"What sort of lady are you looking for anyway? Maybe I can be on the lookout. I was quite a matchmaker in my day."

Is that why you never married? He didn't dare ask the question. "I'm not looking." Truthfully, Colin didn't see the point. When the Lord was ready to bring him a bride, she would simply appear—he prayed.

"That's half your trouble." Ida shook her head. "How can you ever expect to find something if you're not looking for it?"

He shook his head in disbelief. "You sound like my mother."

The older woman broke into a broad smile and slipped her arm into the crook of his as they approached the building. "Why, that's the nicest thing you've ever said to me." She paused and looked up at him intently. "Tell you what," she said with a broad grin, "if neither of us is married in a year, why don't we just bite the bullet and marry each other?"

"Ida," he said, then chuckled. "To be perfectly honest, I don't know if my heart could take it."

ten

Jessica sprinted, nearly breathless, to the baggage claim area of the Dallas–Fort Worth Airport. She managed to locate Nathan standing in the midst of a crowd of people, his hand tightly clutching the handle of his rolling bag. He looked anything but happy. She waved her hand to get his attention and hollered, "Nathan! Over here."

He shook his head as she approached. "This is the craziest excuse for an airport I've ever seen. I can't believe this mob."

Jessica couldn't argue the point. In fact, she had perused the parking garage for nearly half an hour in search of a place to deposit her car. After finally locating a spot, she had walked a good half mile to get to the baggage claim area.

"I was starting to think you'd forgotten about me." Nathan gave her a forced pout.

"How could I forget about you? I love you." She reached up and gave him a playful peck on the cheek. "I've just been stuck in traffic. And the parking situation is terrible. This airport is a mess."

"No kidding." He looked around at the throng of people and shook his head.

They walked hand in hand to the parking garage. Jessica tried to lift his spirits by telling him some of her ideas for the wedding. By the time they arrived at the car, he seemed to be far more relaxed. His broad smile let her know everything was right with the world once again.

"So, what's the plan for tonight?" he asked.

"It's going to be so wonderful." Jessica came alive with excitement. "All of the children are going to be there, along with nearly three hundred financial supporters of the program. The kids will be sharing one of the songs from the production. But don't get your hopes up too high." She paused as she thought about the anxiety level of the children. "We just started rehearsals a couple of weeks ago, and they're still on a learning curve."

Nathan shrugged. "Wouldn't know the difference."

As they climbed into the car, Jessica continued. "We'll be going back to my apartment first to get changed. Then we'll meet Colin and the others at the theater at six fifteen."

"Colin?" Nathan gave her an awkward glance.

"Sure. He's in charge of tonight's event. Anyway, we'll be meeting him to finalize some plans for the kids, who will arrive at six thirty. Dinner will be served at seven. They tell me it's going to be wonderful."

"No more buffet lines?"

"Nope. This is a sit-down affair. But even if I get busy, you won't be completely alone. My neighbor Kellie will be there."

"Really? Why would she come to something like this? I thought she couldn't stand opera."

"She can't. But her sister, Katie, sings with the company, remember? In fact, she is playing one of the leads in *Madame Butterfly*. I'm sure you'll hear all about it before the night's over. Katie has a tendency to talk your ear off."

"Great."

"When she's not trying to get Colin's attention, that is." Jessica smiled as she thought about Katie's ridiculous antics to win the attentions of the man she called, "Verdi himself!" Colin was either blind or not interested. He didn't seem to pay much attention to the vivacious blond, though she fought with every ounce of strength to be noticed.

Jessica continued to fill Nathan in on the details as she drove. By the time they arrived at her apartment, they had just enough time to quickly change into evening attire and prepare to leave once again. Jessica had selected a new dress for the occasion and could hardly wait to show it off. As she entered the living room in the sage green gown with beaded straps, she awaited Nathan's response.

"What time did you say we have to be there?" He stared at his reflection in the mirror as he straightened his tie.

"Six fifteen."

He turned her direction but seemed to see right through her. "Shouldn't we be going then?"

Jessica glanced at her watch. They should have just enough time if she hurried. She tightened a bobby pin to hold a loose hair in place, then smiled at Nathan. "I'm ready when you are."

Jessica was on pins and needles as she drove to the theater. She tried to envision how the evening would go—how she would comfortably work Nathan into all of her plans. The last thing she wanted was to make him feel left out. She would make sure that didn't happen.

Jessica pulled the car into the parking garage at 6:13. "We need to make a run for it." Hand in hand, they raced toward the beautiful lobby, where carefully decorated tables with elaborate centerpieces had been set up ahead of time. Once inside, Jessica couldn't help noticing Nathan's look of admiration.

"This is quite a place," he said.

"I know." She sighed. "It's beautiful here." She located a place for the two of them to sit and asked Nathan to wait for her while she tried to track down the children. Jessica fought her way through the ever-growing crowd heading in the direction of the rehearsal room at the south end of the lobby. She found herself distracted on more than one occasion by chatty new friends, who all enthusiastically told her how lovely she looked. She thanked them all and tried to keep moving, though she couldn't seem to locate Colin anywhere.

Lord, don't let him be late. I can't do this by myself. As if in direct answer to her prayer, she made him out through the crowd. In his sleek black tuxedo, he almost looked like a character from a movie. His dark curls seemed a little less unruly tonight, and his cheeks were flushed with excitement as he talked to a friend. Though she certainly didn't intend to, Jessica found herself staring. *He's really in his element.*

Just then, her neighbor Katie approached with a curious smile on her face. "That fiancé of yours is quite a catch," she said with an admiring grin.

"Oh, you met him?" Jessica glanced back at Nathan, who still sat alone. He looked bored out of his mind and, for a brief moment, she regretting leaving him.

"Sure did," Katie said. "Interesting first meeting, I don't mind telling you."

"What do you mean?"

Her friend giggled. "He thought I was Kellie. Called me by the wrong name."

"Oh."

"I played along with him," Katie said. "But do you know what he said to me?"

Jessica shook her head.

"He told me he'd rather be watching C-Span. Wanted to know if I felt the same way." Katie laughed.

Jessica's heart sank. "You're kidding."

The blond shook her head. "Nope. Then he made some sort of joke about music. I take it he's not an opera fan?"

"I'm working on him." Jessica bit her lip as she stared at Nathan once again.

"Still, he's a cutie," Katie said admiringly. "With a face like that, who needs to like opera?"

Jessica looked up to see Kellie approaching her fiancé. What appeared to be a look of relief crossed his face. He immediately dove into animated conversation with Katie's beautiful twin sister. *Why can't he light up like that when we're talking?*

"Jess, are you with me?" Katie looked at her curiously.

"Oh, yeah." She turned her attention back to her friend. "I'm just a little preoccupied. But I need to stay focused. I need to connect with Colin quickly so we can get the kids ready."

"I happen to know right where he is." Katie's face lit up. "Let me take you to him. It will give me an excuse to spend some time with him. You don't mind, do you?"

"Of course not." Together they pressed their way through the crowd to Colin's side.

He looked up with a broad smile as they approached. "Wow." He gave an admiring whistle. "Must be my lucky night. You both look exceptionally gorgeous."

"Thank you, kind sir." Katie curtsied, and he bowed in response.

"And, I might say," Colin turned in Jessica's direction, "that shade of green is exquisite with your beautiful auburn hair, Miss Chapman." He gestured for her to turn around, and she did so with an embarrassed flush.

"You flatter me." She extended her hand, and he kissed it with a theatrical flair. For a moment, Jessica could hardly breathe. *Stop it. He's just playacting*.

Katie cleared her throat and extended her hand, as well. Colin repeated the gesture, though his gaze never seemed to leave Jessica. She felt her cheeks warm and wondered what he might be thinking. "I, uh, thought we should probably meet with the children soon." She glanced at her watch.

"You're right. Let's get a head count then take a few minutes to run through the first part of their piece as a warm-up."

She nodded and attempted to stop the butterflies that suddenly seemed to fill her stomach.

"Are you okay?" Katie nudged her.

"Yes, why?"

"I don't know." Her friend looked at her nervously. "You're a little flushed."

"Oh," Jessica stammered. "It's warm in here—that's all. I'll be better off when we get to the rehearsal room. I'm sure it's cooler in there."

"Do you need my help?" Katie's lips turned down in a rehearsed pout as she looked back and forth between Colin and Jessica.

"I think we'll be fine," he said, "but thanks for the offer." He turned to face Jessica. "Are you ready?"

She smiled her response, and they moved through the crowd together.

જે

Colin couldn't seem to wipe the silly grin off of his face all evening. He directed the children as they sang one of their selections from *Amahl and the Night Visitors* in front of three hundred excited patrons. Though they struggled a bit in one small section, the youngsters did a fabulous job, in spite of any obstacles. With only a few days' rehearsal under their belts, even the adult company would have found the complicated piece a challenge.

And Jessica. . .

Colin couldn't be prouder of his new coworker. She led the children through their brief rehearsal and cheered them on with a vengeance. When she stood before the crowd to introduce the youth program, she did so with dramatic flair, drawing both the chuckles and sighs of those in attendance. All night long, she remained his fiercest ally. Colin overheard many excited comments about her participation, and he knew beyond a shadow of a doubt that God had certainly brought her to Dallas for such a time as this.

As the evening drew to a close, he caught a glimpse of Jessica from across the room. She stood, arm in arm, with her fiancé. *I need to get to know Nathan better. I'm sure he's a great guy. He'd have to be, to win her heart.*

A giggly female voice interrupted his thoughts. "What are

you thinking about?" He turned to face Katie. She was all smiles, as usual.

"Not much," he said thoughtfully. "I'm just so proud of the kids."

"You have a lot to be proud of. They did a great job." She took his arm and looked up into his eyes longingly. "You've done a terrific job with them, Colin."

"I, uh. . .thank you." He gazed into Katie's bright blue eyes and noticed, for the first time, how they sparkled with joy. The two entered into a lively conversation about the children, and Colin felt himself relax a little. *She's a great girl. Why am I trying so hard not to like her?* For some reason, he immediately thought of Ida and wondered what she would think of Katie. Would she approve?

From across the room, a burst of joyful laughter rose above the cacophony of sounds. His breath caught in his throat as Jessica captured his attention. As she played with one of the little girls, her rich auburn hair slipped out of the barrette and bounced across her shoulders. Her green dress shimmered under the room's subtle lights and brought out the rich glow in her face. Bright freckles seemed more pronounced than ever across those flushed cheeks.

For whatever reason, Colin couldn't seem to take his eyes off of her.

eleven

Jessica sat in the spacious Dallas Opera House and lost herself in her own imagination. Like the Wortham Theater in Houston, this room also seemed to call out to her with its carved walls and sweeping stairways. The stage loomed before her, beckoning. She trembled slightly as she glanced over her music one last time.

Jessica's formal audition for the Dallas Metropolitan Opera would take place in a few short minutes. Colin had assured her position with the organization, even going so far as to offer their letter of acceptance in advance. However, this audition would serve to meet the requirements of her contract. Regardless, she still felt oddly unsure of herself today.

Jessica took slow, deep breaths and tried to relax. *Father, I place this into Your hands. Surely You wouldn't bring me this far to turn me back around now.* She tried to relax as she leaned back against the plush velvet stadium seat. She glanced to her right, where Colin stood visiting with the opera director, Eugene Snyder. The balding, middle-aged man had made a brief appearance at the fund-raiser dinner, sweeping in just long enough to hear the children sing. Even then, he seemed to look down his long, thin nose at her, and she felt strangely uncomfortable around him already. However, Colin gave her an assuring smile, and her nerves began to calm.

Jessica turned her attention to her left. The gilded balconies seemed to rise almost to the sky. *I wonder what the view is like from up there.* She glanced up at the stage where she would soon stand to sing. Its broad wooden floor seemed to stretch forever across the vast expanse of the theater's front side. A retractable orchestra pit loomed before it. Though empty at the time, Jessica could imagine the area filled with violins, cellos, and French horns. The instrumentalists would play something beautiful, something familiar. . . .

The wedding march. They would play the wedding march as she entered from the back of the theater, dressed in an eye-catching chiffon gown she had designed herself. *Did I dream all of this?* She would make her way across a carefully designed bridge to the stage, where her anxious groom would await. With the minister, of course.

A beautiful set would frame the back of the stage. Florence itself would come to life. Cobblestone streets. . . Antiquated homes. . . Fountains and storefronts would provide the perfect backdrop for the most blissful of all wedding ceremonies. She and Nathan would be married between large, draped columns in the center of the stage.

Nathan. Hmm.

Jessica sighed quietly as she roused herself from the daydream. *It was only a dream, anyway. Don't make too much of it.* Her fiancé would never agree to a wedding like the one she envisioned now. *If I even suggested getting married onstage, he would probably*—

"Miss Chapman?"

Jessica looked up into Mr. Snyder's narrow, gray eyes. "Yes, sir?"

"I'm ready to hear you sing now."

She approached the stage with her knees knocking against each other. *Keep me calm, Father.* From a distance, Colin urged her on with a wink and a smile. The whole thing felt slightly reminiscent of her audition in Houston just a short time ago. Entering the stage seemed to boost her courage, and once she faced the auditorium, the butterflies all but disappeared.

As Jessica began to sing, the whole world seemed to close in around her. Once again, she found herself in that private place, that safe haven. Nothing—no one—could disturb her here. When the song ended, she turned her attention to Mr. Snyder, who looked at her with renewed interest.

"Very nice, Miss Chapman. I'll have no trouble placing you in our current production. Welcome to the Met."

"Thank you, sir." She made her way to the edge of the stage and shook his outstretched hand. His eyes shone with excitement.

"In case I haven't said it before," he added, "we at the Dallas Metropolitan Opera would like to thank you for all of your work with the children. Colin here tells me you're doing a magnificent job."

"Did he?" She felt her lips turn up as she looked at her coworker.

"He did." Mr. Snyder looked at his watch then turned on his heels, still talking as he walked away. "And I was fortunate enough to catch a glimpse of the two of you in action the other night with those children. Terrific work, and in such a short time, too."

"Thank you." Jessica could hardly contain her joy.

"I'd love to chat with you again soon, Miss Chapman." He stopped and glanced over his shoulder at her. "I'm sorry, but I'm late for a luncheon now." With little more than a quick "good-bye," he sprinted from the room.

"Nice to meet you, sir." Her voice echoed across the theater. Jessica turned to face Colin once again. "Thanks for the compliment," she whispered.

He shrugged. "I didn't make it up, you know. You're great with those kids, Jessica. You seem to truly relate to them."

"I *do* relate to them." Jessica felt her excitement growing. "I know how important it is for young musicians to have the moral support of a grown-up. When I was a little girl. . ." She paused as she debated whether to continue.

Colin gave her a reassuring nod. "Go ahead."

"When I was a little girl," she continued, "my father made sure I had both a piano and private music lessons. It was a sacrifice on his part. I know that now." A lump rose in her throat as she remembered her father's loving voice. *You'll wow them all someday, honey. Just wait and see.* At the time, her fingers had nervously trembled across unfamiliar keys. Now they seemed to sail. "He really poured so much into my life," she said. "And when he died. . ." Her voice broke. Jessica fought to regain her composure. "When he died, I thought I'd lost the music forever. It seemed to disappear with him."

"I'm so sorry." Colin looked at her sympathetically. "I had no idea you'd lost your father."

She nodded and wiped away a loose tear. "It was nearly a year before I touched the piano again. When I did, God used the music to heal my broken heart. And then the words came. I started to sing and couldn't seem to stop."

"You mean you had never trained as a vocalist?" He looked stunned.

"Never. I was a freshman in college when I stumbled into my first voice lesson. To be honest, the whole process nearly scared me out of my wits. I can't believe I stuck with it. But my mom was there to support me. And Andrew. He and my mother haven't been married very long, but he really has been like a father to me."

Colin gazed at her with a new light in his eyes. "That's great, Jess."

"Yeah. He's been great," she said. "They've all been very supportive. But my grandmother. . ." Jessica's words took on a new life as she began to pour out the story of all her grandmother had done in recent days to assure her move to Dallas.

"I'm awfully glad you took her advice," Colin said as she finished the tale.

"Me, too." Jessica gave a relieved giggle. "It took me long enough though."

"Nah. You were right on time."

She gazed into his eyes and, for the first time, Jessica truly noticed what a rich shade of brown they were. Her cell phone rang out, and she quickly fetched it from her purse. "I can't believe I forgot to turn this off," she said. "I'm glad it didn't go off during the audition."

Colin turned away to give her some privacy as she pulled the phone from her purse. Jessica's excitement grew as she looked at the screen. *Nathan. I can't wait to tell him!*

"Jess, is that you?"

Her heart lifted at the sound of his voice. "It's me."

"How did your audition go?"

"Great." She dove into a full explanation. When she reached the part about her conversation with Colin afterward, Nathan grew oddly quiet.

"Are you still there?" she asked.

"Uh-huh."

"Is something wrong?" Her heart fluttered in anticipation of his response.

"It's just that Colin guy," Nathan said. "Something about him bugs me. Are you having trouble figuring out that he likes more than your voice?"

"Nathan, that's crazy." She had never considered the possibility. Colin Phillips was a great guy, to be sure, but he had been a perfect gentleman in every way. He certainly knew about her relationship with Nathan and had never indicated any interest in her other than their musical working relationship. "I think you're reading too much into things," she spoke nervously into the cell phone. "And besides, you've got nothing to worry about. I'm going to be your wife soon, and that's the important thing."

After a long pause, he spoke. "I know." A deep sigh framed his next words. "I guess I'm just feeling the pain of this separation. When are you coming home, Jess?"

"Weekend after next." She glanced at her watch. "But right now, I have to let you go. I'm late for a rehearsal. I'll call you tonight."

"That won't work. I've got a meeting."

"Tomorrow at one?"

"I'll be in class."

She groaned. "Well, I'll connect with you as soon as I can. I've really got to get off of here now. The kids are waiting. I love you, honey."

"I love you, too." The line went dead, and she closed her phone with a click then sprinted toward the rehearsal room.

☙

As Colin made his way across the front of the rehearsal room, he pondered Jessica's story about her father. *No wonder she takes such an interest in the children. There's a lot more to Jessica Chapman than I knew.* He silently thanked the Lord, once again, for bringing someone so miraculous and kind to fill this position.

Just as he turned to face the crowd of children, she made a breathless entrance. "Sorry I'm late."

"No problem."

They carried on with the rehearsal, and everything went well. The talented group managed to perfect the song they had performed at the fund-raiser and start another without much difficulty. Colin continued to marvel at Jessica's ability to get the children to listen and obey with enthusiasm. *How does she do that?*

When the session ended and the children scattered to the winds, he and Jessica were left alone in the large room. Colin turned his attention to a pressing matter. "I wanted to ask your opinion on something." He gazed into her wide, green eyes, still sparkling with excitement from her work with the children.

"Sure." She pulled up a chair and sat down.

"I'm trying to decide which spring production to choose for the kids."

"Ah."

"I've been thinking about *The Magic Flute*."

She wrinkled her nose. "Too overdone."

"*Hansel and Gretel*?"

"Kind of scary for children," she said with a shrug.

"Yeah, I guess you're right."

"It's not one of my favorites," she added. "But it's your call."

"What would you suggest?" He truly wanted to hear her opinion on the matter.

"Hmm." Jessica seemed to lose herself in her thoughts for a moment. "What about *The Left-Behind Beasts*? Have you seen it?"

He shook his head. "Nope."

"Great kids' piece based on Noah and the ark. Terrific humor elements and challenging musical pieces. But not too challenging."

He looked at her admiringly. "Sounds perfect. Can you track down a copy of the libretto?"

"Of course."

"Eugene needs an answer by the weekend so he can put his stamp of approval on it. I hardly slept at all last night trying to come up with something," Colin confided.

"You should have called me," she said with a yawn. "I was up."

"At two o'clock in the morning?"

Jessica nodded. "I had a hard time sleeping, too. But I wasn't thinking about opera. For a change."

"Wedding plans?"

"Not really." She shrugged. "I'm not sure what was bothering me. I just couldn't seem to rest. I guess I'm just too excited about the kids. They're so great. Still, I know that they have to go home to less-than-desirable circumstances. That really bothers me. I want to do so much more for them." She began to talk in earnest about the children, and her eyes glistened with a renewed shimmer.

"You're a godsend, Jessica," he said when she finished. "I don't know if I've ever really told you that, but you are definitely an answer to prayer. And I can tell you love the kids—really love them. That's so important."

Her smile broadened. "I do." She gazed at Colin with admiration. "You've led by example. And, in case I haven't said it enough, thank you so much for everything you've done for me. I don't know when anyone's ever taken such a risk with a newcomer like you have. Especially after all I put you through back in Houston. But I'm honored you chose me. I don't know if I've expressed that adequately."

"You don't understand, Jessica," Colin said from his heart, driven by the conviction that her arrival in Dallas had little, if anything, to do with himself. "I didn't choose you."

"You didn't?" She gave him an adorable little pout that, for some bizarre reason, nearly sent his heart through the roof.

Colin looked intently into her eyes as he spoke in earnest. "The fact of the matter is—God chose you."

twelve

The following Sunday evening Colin handed out copies of Christmas music to the elderly choir members at church. Though the holidays were still weeks away, he knew how long it would take to pull this mishmash group of vocalists into shape.

As he handed Ida a copy of "O Holy Night," she looked at him suspiciously. "You're not going to make me sing the solo in this one again, are you?" she asked.

"I was counting on it, Ida," he said. "The Christmas program wouldn't be the same if you didn't."

"I told you last year I wouldn't do it again. Haven't changed my mind." She pressed the music back into his hand.

Colin groaned. The woman's stubbornness could be endearing at times, but this was not one of them. With opera rehearsals heating up, the children's production plowing forward, and so many Christmas carols to be learned, he had far too much on his plate to bicker over technicalities.

"I was thinking of someone younger taking over for me." The older woman placed her stocky hands on her hips and peered at him over the rim of her narrow spectacles.

"Younger?" He looked around the room at the white-haired group. "Did you have someone particular in mind?"

"We were thinking," Walter piped up, "that—"

"Whoa, whoa! What's with this 'we' business? Have you all been conspiring against me?" Colin looked at them in surprise as they began to murmur among themselves. "Well?"

"It's like this, Colin," Ida explained. "We're not getting any younger here. It's about time we had an infusion of youth. We were thinking that one of your lady friends up at the opera might like to take over my solo this year."

"Lady friends?"

"Sure. What about that gal—the one who came up from Houston?"

"Jessica?"

"Jessica." Ida looked mighty pleased with herself as she continued. "I've heard you say she has a lovely voice. Well, why not get her in here to help us out? And bring along a few others, as well."

Colin scratched his head as he pondered her request. "Folks," he said finally, "you don't understand. The Dallas Metropolitan Opera is a professional organization with a paid staff. I couldn't expect vocalists of that caliber to perform for free."

"So much for the Christmas spirit," Walter mumbled.

"Besides," Colin said, choosing to ignore the comment, "the Met is in a production of its own right now. We're up to our earlobes in rehearsals. On top of that, in case I forgot to mention it, I'm helping with a children's Christmas production. This is a very busy season."

"Humph." Ida pursed her lips then spoke her mind, as always. "I know you'll miss hearing me sing. A part of me will miss doing it. I've sung that same carol for twenty years now. But I'm looking forward to passing the opportunity on to someone else. It's as simple as that. I'm not saying I *won't* sing. I'm just saying I don't *want* to sing the solo." She sat with a thud and crossed her arms in marked victory.

Colin shook his head in disbelief.

"Well?" Walter asked.

"I'm thinking." How could he ask Jessica to give more of her time when she had already stretched herself so thin? On the other hand, with so many anxious eyes peering at him now, how could he not?

৯

Jessica sat at the computer late Sunday evening, doing her

best to communicate with her fiancé online. "What do you think of the ivory dishes with the dark green trim?" She typed the words into the tiny box on her computer screen and clicked the SEND icon.

"They're okay," Nathan responded. "Not really my cup of tea, no pun intended."

She chuckled. All evening, the couple had bantered back and forth across the Internet, trying to decide which china and crystal patterns to choose. He felt strongly about solid white; she tended to gravitate toward rich colors.

"Come on, Nathan," she typed. "I've been looking at this stuff for days." Not that she really minded. In fact, shopping for the wedding always brought a familiar comfort. And she felt great about the fact that she had narrowed her fine china list to three or four possibilities. Katie and Kellie had even climbed aboard the wedding registration bandwagon, and together, they had chosen beautiful patterns. But Nathan didn't seem to like any of them.

"Do we really have to have china?" he asked. "What's the point?"

"It's expected." It might not make much sense to ask people to purchase something so seemingly frivolous to a young couple, but she could envision setting the table—a heavy, dark table—with beautiful dishes and crystal goblets. Even if it meant only getting a few pieces now and adding more at a later date, when they could justify it.

"When would we ever use this stuff? Can't we just buy paper plates?"

She smiled at his illogical attempt at humor. "We'll use it, I promise," she typed. Jessica could think of all sorts of occasions for beautiful dishes. Now that she had connected with so many new people, she could see inviting them to dinner, hosting parties, even catering special events for the parents of the children she had grown to love. *Stop thinking like that.*

You're not going to live in Dallas.

"I guess."

"And we still need to decide on flatware." She began to open a new Web site, anxious to move on. "Let's not forget that."

"What's flatware?"

Jessica groaned. She had already sent him links to three sites so that he could be choosing. "Knives and forks. The everyday stuff."

"Oh." For a moment neither of them typed a thing. Finally, a message came through from his end. "Can we change the subject for a minute?"

"Sure." She leaned back in her chair and rubbed at her eyes. After an evening of looking through Web pages, they ached.

"I want to talk to you about something serious."

Jessica braced herself. Already, two times this week, he had broached the topic of their long-distance relationship, and never from a positive standpoint.

"What's up?" she asked.

"My fingers are tired, for one thing," he responded. "And I'm not getting much sleep now that our only form of communication is over the Internet. I can't type as fast as I can talk, and this is wearing me out. My fingers will be thin before this is over."

Jessica sighed loudly. "I know," she typed. "But I can't use my cell phone until the end of the month. I'm already over my minutes."

"This is just such a bummer," he wrote. "Is it worth it, Jess? Are you really happy up there?"

She leaned back in the chair, deep in thought. *I wish he hadn't picked this weekend to ask that question.* The last few days had been rough. Despite Mr. Snyder's assurances, she felt oddly out of place amidst so many competitive vocalists in the adult company. "I'm happy." She took her time typing the words. "It's not everything I hoped it would be, but I still love it."

"I'm just lonely without you."

Jessica's eyes watered immediately. "Me, too." Her heart suddenly felt as if it would burst, and tears started to flow. *Lord, have I made a mistake? I miss him so much, and this is harder than I thought it would be. A lot harder.*

"I'm busy, and that's a good distraction," he wrote. "But something about all of this just seems wrong. Off. Haven't you noticed?"

Not until tonight. "I don't know, Nathan."

"I'm probably just tired. I haven't slept much this week. My workload at school is crazy, and I'm drowning at the office, too."

"Well, we should wrap this up so you can get some sleep then," she typed. "We really need to register online tonight, if we can."

He didn't respond, and Jessica wondered for a moment if he had dozed off.

"So, which pattern would you like?" She typed the words carefully.

"I don't really care, to be honest," he responded. "Why don't you just pick something?"

"Are you sure?" *That would be so much easier.*

"Yeah. I really need to sign off. My dad needs to check his e-mail. But I'll talk to you tomorrow night."

"Same time, same station?" she asked.

"Right."

"I love you," she typed.

"Back at ya."

He disappeared, and she closed out the message screen. With determined zeal, Jessica turned her attention to the department store Web site, where she quickly selected china, crystal, and flatware. The whole process took about ten minutes. When she finished, she clicked the computer off with a satisfied smile and turned her attention, once again, to her music.

thirteen

"Okay, kids. Let's settle down and get to work." Colin wiped a bit of perspiration from his brow as he faced the room full of boisterous children. "Miss Chapman has an announcement to make this afternoon."

His coworker approached the center of the room, all smiles. "I'm happy to report," she said, "that every member of the youth chorus will be given four free tickets to see the Metropolitan's performance of *Madame Butterfly* in two weeks."

The kids reacted with cheers, and Colin smiled at their enthusiasm.

"Are you really playing the lead, Mr. Phillips?" one of the boys asked.

He nodded, suddenly feeling a crater in the pit of his stomach. Just two weeks to pull it all together. To be honest, the Met's upcoming production had already taxed him beyond belief, and with such a short time until opening night, he was certainly feeling the heat. *Why did I agree to carry such a heavy load when my heart is here with these kids?* And yet he knew the answer. His heart was also set on the stage, where he could share the gift God had given him with full abandon.

How could he possibly complain, at any rate? The Lord had given Colin the opportunity of a lifetime this year—carrying his first real lead in a professional company and directing the children—all at the same time.

It was the "all at the same time" that seemed to be giving him fits right now. *I think I'm just tired. If Jessica hadn't come, I don't know what I would have done.* He glanced across the room at his enthusiastic counterpart. The autumn sunlight streamed through the window and picked up the color in her hair, dancing it across the room. For a brief moment, it held him captive. Then, a youngster's giddy voice interrupted his reverie.

"You're the best singer I've ever heard," twelve-year-old Melissa Grover said with a dreamy-eyed giggle.

Colin tried to squelch the preteen's enthusiasm, though he noticed Jessica nodding her agreement from across the room. "I appreciate the compliment," he said, "but I still have a lot to learn, just like all of you. Trust me."

"Don't let Mr. Phillips fool you, kids." Jessica stepped to the center of the room. "He might still be on a learning curve, but he's the best baritone I've ever heard, and I've heard a lot of them."

Colin's cheeks immediately warmed, and he winked his appreciation.

"Thank you, Miss Chapman." He bowed with great dramatic flair.

"You're more than welcome." She saluted in his direction, and the kids laughed.

Jessica's voice rang out above their very vocal response. "Okay, now. It's time to settle down. I have another announcement to make."

Colin watched with amazement as she managed to quiet them down with her playful, singsong voice. "The youth chorus has been asked to do three extra performances of our Christmas production."

The kids erupted in lively conversation, and Colin tried once again to bring the noise level down to a dull roar.

Jessica filled the children in on the details. "We'll be performing at the Old City Park in the historical district. And we'll also be adding two performances at a large church on the south end of town. Then, of course, we'll have our regular performances on the dates we've already discussed. I've got all of the information right here." She waved a stack of papers.

"You'll need to get this information into your parents' hands as soon as possible."

The children swarmed her like flies, and Colin immediately dove into action. "Careful, careful!" He made his way through the crowd and took the papers from Jessica's outstretched hand. As their fingers brushed, she seemed to blush slightly, and the freckles on her cheeks became even more pronounced. *They always do that when she's happy.*

Her eyes glistened with excitement as she spoke. "I have more to tell you," Jessica continued. "But only if you're all sitting down quietly." With a little more encouragement, the children took their papers from Colin, then sat in their seats with looks of curiosity on their faces. "Mr. Phillips has some exciting news for those of you who want to learn a little more about the process of singing."

She gave a grand bow to usher him to the center of the room. The children stirred in their seats. Colin couldn't help smiling as he spoke. "I'm happy to announce that the Dallas Metropolitan Opera has agreed to offer free individual vocal lessons to those of you in the youth program, beginning next Thursday afternoon."

The room grew quite loud once again, and he raised his hands to quiet them. "Now that Miss Chapman's here we have the best vocal instructor in the world on our team." He gestured toward her, and the kids cheered.

Jessica's cheeks immediately reddened. "You flatter me too much, Mr. Phillips." She turned to face the children, and her enthusiasm seemed to grow. "But I am excited to be able to have this opportunity, and I can't wait to schedule your lessons. So, as soon as we finish up today, come and see me to arrange a time."

The voices of the students rose again, and Colin moved forward into the rehearsal, handing the reins off to Jessica, who took charge with her usual grace and flair. She managed to lead the children through more of the material than he had planned, which certainly eased his mind. *Maybe all of those extra performances won't be such a challenge after all.*

When the session with the children ended, Jessica remained behind to clean up the room. She seemed to be in a particularly chatty mood this afternoon. In fact, she talked nonstop as she pushed folding chairs back into tidy rows.

"I had a great time today. These kids are amazing," he said.

"Yes, they are." Then her smile faded somewhat. "Oh, by the way, I just wanted to remind you that I'll be out of town this weekend."

"That's what I figured. How are your wedding plans coming along?"

She looked at him with an alarmed expression. "We're behind schedule, to be honest. We still haven't ordered invitations. I was supposed to be taking care of that the last time I went home."

"Really? Would you like the name of the guy who prints all of our programs for the Met?" he asked. "He's really good. And he's a graphic artist, so he can pretty much do anything you need."

"Is he reasonable?"

"I'm sure he'll give you a break since you work for us."

Jessica's lips turned up in a smile. "I'll be so relieved to get some of this done, but I have to admit, the children have been a distraction. A good distraction, don't get me wrong. But I've got to stay focused on everything at once."

"Oh, speaking of staying focused. . ." Colin finally worked up the courage to ask the question that had been weighing on his mind all afternoon. "I don't suppose you'd be up to singing a solo at my church a couple of weeks before Christmas."

"What?" Jessica looked stunned, and he immediately regretted asking.

"I'm so sorry."

"No, I'm just surprised, that's all," she said. "I do need to get involved in a church while I'm here. If I hadn't spent every other weekend driving back and forth, I would have done so already. But two weeks before Christmas? Do you think we'll be done with the children's performances by then?"

"Yes. Unless we're asked to add more to their schedule."

"Well. . ." She paused, pursing her lips.

"Listen." Colin waved his hand to dismiss the whole idea. "Please forget I said anything."

"Not so fast, not so fast." She grinned. "What's the song?"

" 'O Holy Night.' "

Jessica's eyes lit up in amazement. "That's my grandmother's favorite. I used to sing it every Christmas back home. Interesting."

"I dare say your church choir back home was probably a little different from the one I'm talking about." He dove into a quick explanation, and Jessica grinned.

"They sound awesome, and I'd be happy to do it, Colin."

"Thanks so much. You'll never know what this means to my little choir."

"My pleasure."

"And back to our original conversation," Colin continued, "I'll be praying that the Lord shows you how to keep everything in balance. In the meantime. . ." He swallowed hard. "Say a couple of prayers for me, too."

"What's up?"

Colin didn't respond for a moment as he struggled to come up with the right words.

"Are you worried about *Madame Butterfly*?" she finally asked.

"Not really worried." He exhaled deeply. "I just hope I didn't bite off more than I can chew. Whatever made me think I could handle two productions less than a month apart?" *The kids' performance would have been enough, but with the adult opera season in full swing. . .*

"You'll do great," she said.

He shrugged. "I'm a little behind on memorizing my music for the second act. And, to be honest, this will be the first time I've ever carried a lead role. Don't know if I mentioned that before. Between you and me, I'm a little—"

"Nervous?"

"Maybe a little. I don't want to disappoint anyone. Snyder. The company. My family."

"I don't see that as a possibility." She smiled. "I don't know if I've mentioned this before, but you don't sound like a rookie. And if there's anything I can do to ease your burden on this end—with the kids, I mean—just let me know."

"You've been great, Jess." He reached out and gave her hand a squeeze. "I don't know what I would have done without you."

For a moment his hand lingered on hers. He withdrew it as he suddenly remembered his other prayer request. "Oh, and one more thing." His voice grew shaky. "I, uh—"

"Yes?"

"I'm thinking of asking someone out." *There, I said it. I've finally spoken the words.*

"Katie?" Jessica broke into a broad grin as he nodded. "I think that's great! She's so much fun, and she's so talented, too, Colin. Whenever I hear the two of you singing together, I can't help thinking about what a cute couple you would make."

Cute? "I don't really know for sure about that, but I guess I'll never know if I don't ask her out."

"Oh, I have a wonderful idea!" Jessica's eyes lit up. "Nathan will be here in a couple of weeks to see *Madame Butterfly*. We should all get together and double-date. It would be a great way to ease him into my world here. And," she said as her eyes grew large with excitement, "to make it even more fun, I should ask my brother and Kellie to come along, too. That way everyone would have a partner. What do you think?"

Colin wasn't sure what to think. Somehow, the idea of going out with Katie seemed a little less appealing now that he had voiced it aloud.

"You'll never know unless you ask her!" Jessica gave him a playful punch in the arm.

He rubbed the spot and gave a thoughtful response. "I guess you're right. I'll never know unless I ask her."

❧

On Saturday morning, Jessica made the familiar drive to Houston. The crisp November day provided an array of colorful distractions as she headed south on Interstate 45. The pine trees on either side of the freeway were usually green and full. Today, they seemed browner, less dense. On some level, they served to remind her that this season of her life would pass far too quickly. All too soon, her time in Dallas would be over.

"I need to stop feeling sorry for myself," she said aloud to the empty car. "I need to be grateful for the time I do have." Jessica chided herself for feeling blue and reaffirmed her commitment to approach everything in her life with both joy and balance.

About the time she passed the midway point in her journey, Jessica's cell phone rang, and she fumbled around inside her purse with one hand to retrieve it. Looking down at the screen, she had to smile. She answered the phone with great enthusiasm. "Grandma, is that you?"

"It's me. Just wondering if you're going to be on time. I'm anxious to get rolling."

Jessica glanced at the clock on her car stereo. "I should be pulling into the Houston area a little after noon. Want to meet me for some pizza before we go shopping?"

"You know pizza's my favorite. And your grandpa Buck never lets me eat it. He thinks it's for kids."

"Kids like me." Jess laughed.

"And me, too. So, what's on the agenda for today?" her

grandmother asked. "Still looking at wedding dresses?"

"Uh-huh. And flowers. Today I just want to get some ideas. Maybe I'll place an order next time. Right now, I don't even know what I'm looking for."

"Good thing I know my flowers, right?"

"Right." Jessica couldn't help smiling. "I know Mom wanted to go with me, but she and Andrew are at some sort of seminar."

"It's that 'Song of Solomon' romance thing up at the church," her grandmother said with a giggle. "I wanted to go myself, but Buck wouldn't hear of it. He figured people would think we had a troubled marriage."

Jessica laughed. "Anyone who knows you would know better. I envy your romance with Buck."

"Thanks, honey," her grandmother said, "but still—I think it would have been fun, and you know, it wouldn't hurt you and Nathan to sign up for something like that before you tie the knot, either."

"I know." Jessica calculated her response. She and Nathan could certainly use some help in the romance department. Bickering seemed to be their primary form of communication these days. "But right now I guess I'd better focus on the big day."

"No point in having a big day without a big life to follow it. And a big life needs a little rehearsal, just like one of your shows."

"I know, I know." Jessica groaned.

"Speaking of your shows, how are rehearsals coming?"

"Great. I can hardly wait for next weekend." Jessica dove into a lengthy discussion about *Madame Butterfly*, thankful for the reprieve from the focus on her love life.

When she finished giving her grandmother the colorful details of all that been happening in Dallas, the elderly woman responded, "Sounds like you're having the time of your life."

"I am. I don't think I've ever been happier."

"That's my girl."

"So. . ." Jessica looked at the clock and realized with some surprise that she had been talking nearly half an hour. "Where would you like to meet for lunch again?"

"Pizza. That all-you-can-eat place in The Woodlands suits me just fine. Just don't tell my hips, okay?"

"I promise."

"Or your grandpa Buck."

Jessica laughed. "No problem." She hung up the phone with a grin on her face. More than an ally and close friend, her grandmother had proven to be a source of comfort over the past few weeks, sending countless e-mails and offering encouragement with words of humor and wisdom. *Thank You, Lord, for blessing me with such a wonderful grandmother.*

As she continued the drive, Jessica thought about all she must accomplish in the next thirty-six hours. *I've got to find a dress, visit with my family, see Nathan. . .* She struggled with the emotions that followed the thought of her fiancé. *Something just feels wrong. Off.* Were those his words or her own? Why did nothing these days seem to feel like it should? *Probably just prewedding jitters. I'm nervous about getting married. That's pretty common.*

As was so often the case, Jessica's thoughts shifted to the goings-on in Dallas. She enjoyed her new life more than she had dared dream. And, at the center of it all stood a friend who towered above her, not just vocally but spiritually, as well. Colin Phillips. A strange mixture of emotions flooded Jessica when she thought about him. She would never have thought to feel guilty about her budding friendship with Colin if Nathan hadn't brought him up time and time again. "He likes more than your voice."

Lord, I'm sure that's not true, she prayed. *But if this friendship is outside Your will, please show me. Then help me figure out a way to avoid any unnecessary contact with Colin. I don't want anything—or anyone—to stop me from Your plan for my life.*

Still, she didn't feel at peace about staying away from the tall, dark-haired songster, either. Colin, perhaps more than anyone else, seemed to understand where she was coming from—not just musically, but emotionally and spiritually, as well.

One day Nathan will understand me like that. In time. When we're married. . .

Jessica couldn't seem to complete her thought. Something about all of this just felt very, very wrong.

fourteen

Colin glanced across the stage at Katie. His palms, damp with sweat, trembled as he approached her. *Easy, man. You're making this harder than it is.* As he drew near, he smelled the intoxicating aroma of her perfume. "Katie." *Why do I sound so insecure?*

She turned to face him and immediately broke into a broad smile. "Colin. What's up?"

"I, uh, I just wanted to talk to you."

"Really? What about?"

"I, um. . ."

"Colin, are you ready?" Eugene Snyder called out to him from the front row of the auditorium. "We're already running late."

Colin glanced at his watch. *Seven forty.*

"What is it?" Katie whispered. Her beautiful blue eyes sparkled with excitement.

"Can you stay after a few minutes?" he whispered back. "I need to talk to you."

She nodded with an impish grin, and Colin's heart began to beat double time. *What is wrong with me? I feel like I'm in high school again.*

He took his place in the center of the stage and tried to prepare himself for the rehearsal. Things started well, but over the course of the next hour and a half, calamity struck several times. He seemed to be off tonight. Way off. His voice cracked and wavered, and his pitch stayed more than a little low.

Eugene Snyder brought the orchestra to a screeching halt. "Colin!"

"Yes?"

"You're flat," the frustrated director called out from across the auditorium.

"I know." Colin groaned. "I'm working on it."

"Well, work harder. We're down to the wire here. In less than a week you'll be standing in front of thousands of patrons who have spent their hard-earned money to hear you sing."

"I know. I know." Colin vowed to do a better job but, for some reason, couldn't seem to get control of his breathing tonight. The orchestra started once again, but things only seemed to get worse. He tried to focus—tried to stay on top of things—but his mind seemed to be playing tricks on him tonight. At one point, just as he reached a high note, he tripped across a loose cable and nearly lost his balance. If Katie hadn't grabbed his arm, he would surely have hit the floor. Out of the corner of his eye, Colin caught a glimpse of Jessica. Her face, etched with concern, held him captive.

All the while, Colin argued with himself. *What are you doing? What is your problem? Are you really hung up on Katie, or are you just kidding yourself?* As the rehearsal drew to a close, he found himself losing his initial courage. *Don't ask her. Don't do it. If she says yes, you'll get caught up in something you're not ready for.*

On the other hand. . .

On the other hand, could this fear be the very thing to keep him from the relationship God had planned for him all along?

There's no way to know if I don't work up the courage to ask her.

After the rehearsal, Katie approached him. "I'm sorry you had such a hard time tonight, Colin." Her lips curved downward in an exaggerated pout. "Old man Snyder can be downright cruel sometimes."

"No, he was right on target. I'm the one who was off."

"You sounded great." Katie shrugged. "I don't know what his problem is. He has no patience."

"Trust me, he was more than patient tonight," Colin said.

"Anyway. . ." She grabbed his arm. "You said you wanted to talk to me. What's up?"

From across the stage, Colin sought out Jessica's face. *Why do I care if she's watching? What difference should that make?* She gave him an encouraging wink and a thumbs-up. He immediately felt every ounce of courage drain out of him. *I can't do this.* He turned to face Katie.

"Yes?"

"I was wondering if you had an extra copy of the opening number from Act Two. I've lost mine." *That's true, anyway.*

Katie's smile immediately faded. "You need a copy of my music?"

"Yeah. If you don't mind." *You're such a coward, Colin.*

"I think I have one." Her face lit up once again. "It's at my place. Would you like to follow me back there? We could fix some coffee and run through the music if you like."

Now what are you going to say? "I, um. . . I'm too tired, to be honest. Could you just bring it tomorrow night instead?"

"Sure. I guess." Her eyes seemed to lose a little of their sparkle.

"Thanks for being such a great friend." He reached out and gripped her hand, and she squeezed his in response.

"See you tomorrow night, music in hand." Katie gave him a girlish wave as she left the stage.

Colin's shoulders sagged in defeat.

"So?" He turned at the sound of Jessica's cheery voice. "Did you ask her?"

"I didn't." His gaze traveled to the floor, where he carefully examined the tops of his shoes.

"Why not?" Jessica crossed her arms, a clear sign of her disappointment.

"I don't know." Colin groaned. "I just couldn't seem to do it. Maybe it was just something about tonight. Everything about me seems to be a little. . ."

"Off?" She chuckled.

"You noticed?"

"Yeah, but don't let it get you down. We all have off nights, trust me. In fact, that's been my word of the week."

&

"I'm exhausted." Jessica spoke through a yawn as she drove Katie home from the rehearsal. "What about you?"

"I'm too excited to be tired," her friend said. "I think Colin's starting to soften up. I hope so, anyway."

"He's such a great guy, Katie. You two would make a perfect couple."

"I agree. But I don't know if I can wait forever. Is he ever going to make his move?"

Jessica pulled onto the interstate as the conversation continued. "I think he's just a little shy. Around women, anyway. But you should see him with the kids. He's very outgoing with them."

"And with you."

Jessica thought she detected a bit of animosity in Katie's voice. "What do you mean?" she asked.

"He's obviously very comfortable around you," Katie said with a shrug. "You two are always laughing and talking together."

Is she jealous? "You know how guys are." Jessica spoke in her most reassuring voice. "They always feel comfortable talking with women they're not attracted to. That's why he's less nervous around me. I'm more like a buddy. A pal. When he's with you. . ." Silence permeated the vehicle for a moment as Jessica fought to complete the sentence. "When he's with you, he's probably a nervous wreck trying to figure out what to say, how to say it. You know."

"I hope."

"I hope, too."

Jessica gripped the steering wheel with both hands and

tried to conquer the doubt that suddenly gripped her. For some inexplicable reason, she felt a little uncomfortable around Katie tonight. *All this time I've been thinking about how good Colin would be for her, but I've never once thought about whether she would be good for him.* Jessica fought to push the nagging doubts from her mind as she focused on the road ahead.

fifteen

When the curtain pulled back on the night of the first *Madame Butterfly* performance, Jessica could hardly contain her emotions. Even from her current position far upstage right, she could hear the whisper of voices and the creaking of chairs as patrons stirred in their seats. *They're anxious. So am I.* She couldn't make out any faces from here, especially not with the blinding lights in her eyes, but somewhere out there sat her family. And Nathan. *He'll be so proud.*

She attempted to press down the lump in her throat, but it wouldn't budge. When it came time to sing, Jessica tried to distract herself. Her hands trembled and, for a moment, she felt as if she might be sick. Finally her nerves steadied themselves, and she released herself to enjoy the experience. *Lord, this is so amazing. Thank You so much.* From the stage, looking out, the whole thing felt more like a dream than reality.

Jessica sang with full release—from the depths of her soul. When she exited the stage for her first costume change, she paused long enough at the backstage entrance to listen to Colin as he completed his first solo. *He's really on tonight. I'm so glad.* The crowd erupted with applause as he hit the final note of the song, and she found herself applauding along with them.

Then Katie's solo began. Jessica stood in awe. The young woman lit the stage with her incredible vocal presence. Jessica looked back and forth between Colin and Katie with a feeling of satisfaction. All of her doubts from the other night seemed to vanish. *They're going to make quite a couple. In every conceivable way.*

"Move please." A stage tech tapped her on the shoulder, and she suddenly remembered where she was—and where she was supposed to be. Jessica quickly scurried back to the changing room and slipped into costume number two.

By the time intermission came, she felt like a pro. Jessica chatted backstage with others in the chorus as she awaited her next entrance. Somehow, the wait felt like an eternity.

As she entered the stage once again, the lights and the swell of the orchestra pulled her into their spell. *Father, I've waited for this moment all my life. This is my passion. This is what You created me to do.* She opened her mouth and began to sing with the others. The joy that enraptured her seemed to take root in her soul, and Jessica knew she would never be the same again.

At one point during the second act, she caught Colin's attention to give him an encouraging nod. He winked at her, and an immeasurable joy gripped her heart. *He's the reason I'm here. He knew. He knew I had to come.* Somehow the realization overwhelmed her. To think, the Lord had gone to such trouble to bring her to Dallas. What if she hadn't listened? What if she had missed all of this?

Jessica never found time to contemplate the matter. The performance came to an end all too quickly. She pressed back tears of relief and excitement as she took her bow alongside others in the cast. When Colin approached center stage, the audience roared. Most of them stood. Jessica didn't blame them and, in fact, clapped until her hands ached.

When the curtain closed, she exited the stage in the stampede of excited vocalists. For a moment, she almost forgot about meeting her family in the foyer—almost forgot the hastily planned dinner at a nearby restaurant.

For now, all she could think about—all that mattered—was the music. Katie approached from her right, and Jessica embraced her tightly. "You were absolutely—without a doubt—the most amazing thing I've ever heard."

"Quite a compliment coming from one of the best voices in the company."

"I mean it, Katie. You were awesome tonight."

"And didn't you think Colin just brought the house down?" Katie squeezed her hands impulsively.

"He was great. I'm totally impressed."

"I just wish he was as brave off the stage as he is on." Katie sighed and pulled off a piece of her costume jewelry.

"He hasn't asked you out yet?"

"Nope. Still waiting." Katie turned to visit with her parents, who had just arrived backstage. The elderly couple offered their congratulations boisterously, clearly proud of their daughter.

Jessica leaned against the back wall, suddenly drained of all strength.

"Jess?" She turned as she heard Colin's resonant voice. "Was it everything you hoped it would be?"

"Oh, Colin. It was. . . It was. . ."

Tears flowed, but she didn't even try to stop them. Jessica reached up to embrace him, then pulled away, embarrassed.

"It's okay," he whispered, his own eyes moist, as well. "I'm feeling it, too."

"You were just wonderful." Jess took his hand. "I've never heard anything like it."

"You flatter me, Miss Chapman." He ran his thumb along her fingers. "But you haven't told me if you liked it. Was the experience everything you hoped it would be?"

"Everything and more!" Jessica could scarcely catch her breath. "I could feel the orchestra, Colin! Not just hear them but feel them. The whole stage seemed to be electric. And when we all sang together, the entire auditorium felt full of music. We weren't just a chorus of strangers singing together. We were a multitude—a heavenly choir. It was the most unbelievable experience of my life." Tears coursed down her cheeks, and she used her fingertips to brush them away.

"I'm so glad. I knew it." He took her hand again. "I knew you would love it."

Yes, he knew. "Thank you for bringing me here," Jessica whispered. Her arms seemed to instinctively reach for his shoulders once again. "I can never thank you enough."

"You're welcome. If anyone deserves this opportunity, you do." He returned her hug with a warm squeeze. "I predict this is just the first of many performances for you."

"Thank you." In his arms, with the crowd pressing in around her, Jessica could barely breathe.

"Jess?" She looked up as she heard another familiar voice. Nathan stood to her left, a puzzled expression on his face.

She pulled away from Colin's embrace with an embarrassed warmth flooding her cheeks. "Nathan! I'm so glad you're here."

"I can see that."

Lord, please don't let him misunderstand. I don't want anything to ruin this wonderful evening.

"Good to see you again, Nathan." Colin extended his hand and, thankfully, Nathan shook it warmly. Colin excused himself and returned to the throng of well-wishers.

Once they were alone, Jessica gazed into her fiancé's eyes for a look of assurance.

"I hope you don't mind that I came backstage." His words seemed a little stilted.

"Of course not. It's wonderful." She slipped her arm around his waist. For some reason, he didn't respond by pulling her close, as usual. Instead, Nathan pressed a bouquet of flowers into her hand.

"These are for you."

"Thank you." Her lips brushed his in thanks.

"Your mom and Andrew are waiting in the foyer," he added.

"Did my grandmother make it? I know she wasn't feeling well a couple of days ago."

"She and Buck are both here. And Kent."

"Looking for Kellie, no doubt."

"He found her." Nathan shook his head. "In fact, she sat with us tonight."

"Really?" Interesting, since the double date idea hadn't panned out. *Maybe God has a few matchmaking plans of His own.*

"How long will it take you to get ready?" Nathan looked at his watch.

"Not long. I'll meet you out front in a couple of minutes." She gave him a peck on the cheek before heading back to the costume room. *He didn't even say if he liked the show or not. I'll have to remember to ask him later.*

Jessica met up with her family in the foyer after the crowd thinned out. They stood in a cluster, with Kent at the center of their conversation. He fought to hold Kellie's attention, though she looked a little distracted at the moment. Nathan interrupted Kent's antics to tell a joke, and everyone laughed. Except Kent.

"I'm here!" Jessica waved her hand triumphantly. Everyone swarmed her at once.

Her mother whispered in her ear, "We're so proud of you. The whole thing was wonderful. Just wonderful."

"I'll bet you had the time of your life up there," Andrew added.

"Oh, I did. It was heaven. Probably one of the highlights of my life."

"That's my girl." Her grandmother slipped her arm around Jess and pulled her into a gentle embrace. "So, was it everything you hoped it would be?" she whispered.

"And more," Jess whispered back. *She knows me so well.*

The family chatted nonstop as they walked the two city blocks to the Italian restaurant Jessica had chosen. She clutched Nathan's hand tightly in hers and silently thanked the Lord for this, the most eye-opening night of her life.

≈

Colin left the theater alone. *Might as well grab a bite to eat on the way home. But where?* Many of the cast members had decided to have a late-night supper at a nearby coffee shop. Somehow that just didn't sound appealing tonight. He looked up as Katie approached. She smiled warmly, and his loneliness vanished almost immediately.

He gave her a warm smile. "Hey, you."

"Hey, you." She reached up and embraced him. "You were awesome tonight, Colin."

"Thanks. You were pretty awesome yourself."

"We make a good team." She gave him a shy look.

Unusual. She seems a little nervous tonight. "Yes." He paused to look into her blue eyes. "We do."

Katie took hold of his hand and squeezed it tightly. "Are you hungry? Would you like to get something to eat?"

"I'm starved," he admitted. *But I would never have the courage to ask you out.*

"There's a great new Italian place a couple of blocks away. It'll probably be pretty quiet. I think everyone else went to the coffee shop."

"Right."

"So. . ."

"I'll tell you what. . ." He took her arm and placed it firmly in his own. "Tonight it's just you, me, and a plate of spaghetti."

She gave him a satisfied grin, and the two walked, arm in arm, to the door. As they made their way to Traviatta's, Colin found himself relaxing. *She's such a great girl. I can't believe I've waited this long to ask her out. Not that I really did the asking, exactly.*

She shivered against the cool evening breeze, and Colin pulled his jacket off. "Here. You take this." He wrapped it around her shoulders, and she looked up with a broad smile.

"You're so thoughtful."

Colin shrugged.

"I'm so glad we're finally going to get this chance to get to know each other," Katie said. "Without the whole group looking on, I mean."

"Me, too." Colin pulled the door of the restaurant open and immediately found himself in a whirlwind of activity. *Great. This place is packed.* From across the room, he heard the sound of laughter.

"Hey, that's my sister!" Katie squealed. "Go figure. And there's that guy she keeps talking about."

"Guy? What guy?" Colin's gaze followed her pointing finger to the table where Jessica's entire family sat, engaged in joyous conversation. "Oh, Jessica's brother?"

"No," Katie whispered in his ear. "Actually, that's not the one she's interested in." She gave a light giggle.

"Excuse me?" Colin peered at the group a little closer. "Who else is there?"

Katie jabbed him in the ribs and nodded her head in a direction that left him without any doubt.

Nathan. Kellie is falling for Jessica's fiancé.

sixteen

For days, Jessica floated around on a cloud of pure adrenaline. She walked herself through the performance time and time again. Each thrilling note had held her in its grasp. Her role in the chorus of *Madame Butterfly* had served not only to boost her confidence; it opened a whole new world of possibilities.

Every now and again she would wonder why a bit of guilt would seep in and catch her unawares. *Why should I feel bad about doing something I love so much?* Perhaps, she reasoned, it was because of Nathan's lack of enthusiasm. The morning following the performance, he had brushed a kiss across her cheek and scurried off to the airport.

Her grandmother, on the other hand, had offered enough support for a dozen people. "You were born for this," she had whispered in Jess's ear after the show. "And your father would have been so proud of you."

As the days rolled by, Jessica found strength in those words. She moved forward with plans for the children's production, though staying focused wasn't an easy task.

An unexpected call came late one Thursday afternoon, just as she pulled her car out of the parking garage at the opera house. At first, she could barely make out her mother's frantic words. Finally, however, she managed to pull a few key phrases from the conversation, enough to send her thoughts and heart reeling.

Grandmother. Stroke. Probably won't pull through.

Through a haze of tears, Jessica now fought her way beyond the crowd of people at the Dallas airport. Colin moved alongside her, his shadow towering over Jessica and offering an odd sense of comfort. When they reached the security gate, her arms went to his neck immediately. They stood in silence for a moment, and she could feel his heartbeat.

"I can't thank you enough," she said. "I never would have made it here in my car."

"No problem." He held her in a warm, brotherly embrace. She trembled in his arms and whispered a frantic prayer for her grandmother as she rested her head against his broad chest. When she pulled away, the tears ran in rivulets down her cheeks, an uncorked bottle of grief.

"I'll be praying." Colin spoke in a reassuring voice as he squeezed her hands. "God's still on the throne, Jess."

"I know." She forced a weak smile. Jessica then stumbled through the security process in a numb fog and boarded the plane for Houston. As she took her seat on the 747, she released herself to the emotion, allowing gut-wrenching sobs to emanate. Never mind the guy in the seat next to her. Never mind the flight attendant with her niceties. *Lord, my grandmother! Don't take her from me, Father. Please!*

The flight seemed to last for hours, though her watch ticked by the forty-five-minute flight with uncanny accuracy. By the time she arrived at Houston's hectic Bush Intercontinental Airport, Jessica felt a heaviness she could not explain. Somehow, she knew. She just knew. *Grandma is gone.*

Her brother met her at the baggage claim area, his face ashen. Though he never spoke a word, Jessica read the truth in his somber expression.

"I'm too late." She whispered the words, and his eyes swiftly brimmed over.

Kent nodded then reached to hug her. "Jess." As he pressed his arms around her, she shook with sobs. By the time she stopped, Jessica felt completely drained. Her eyes stung unmercifully, and her chest ached. All of the tears in the world couldn't make her feel any better.

"Where do we go from here?" she asked.

"Everyone left the hospital about fifteen minutes ago," Kent explained. "Mom and Andrew have gone home to rest. They were up all night. I doubt they'll get much sleep, though. Mom was pretty shook-up."

"Bad?"

He nodded. "The whole thing was just such a shock. Came from out of nowhere."

"What about Buck?" A lump rose in Jessica's throat as she thought of her grandfather and the pain he must be feeling right now.

"He's at our place." Kent reached out and took her bag. "For now, anyway. Mom insisted. He'll have to go home later on to track down some life insurance papers and other stuff, but for now, he's with us."

Jessica nodded then followed her brother out to the parking garage in silence. *She's gone. The one person who understood me best in the world is gone.* She suddenly felt guilty for thinking such a thing. *How can I be so self-centered?*

As they climbed into Kent's car, Jessica reached for her cell phone. She quickly dialed Nathan's number. *I've got to talk to him. He needs to know.* The phone rang several times. Finally the recorded message kicked in. "This is Nathan. Leave a message at the beep, and I'll get back to you."

I can't do it. I can't tell him in a recorded message. She snapped the phone shut and leaned her head against the seat in quiet desperation.

&

About twenty-four hours after Jessica left for Houston, a chill settled over the Dallas area. Unseasonably cold weather locked the city in its grip. Colin fought to continue his work as if nothing had happened. He struggled with his feelings as he waited to hear something, anything, from Jessica. *Should I call? Send an e-mail?* Anything at this point seemed like a better option than waiting, not knowing. For some reason, every time he thought about her, a pain gripped his heart.

Colin shivered against the cold as he crossed the parking lot after Friday's rehearsal with the children. In spite of Jess's absence, they had excitedly tried on their costumes and rehearsed their more difficult numbers. With a show in less than two weeks, Colin had his work cut out for him. Especially if Jessica found herself unable to return.

Ironically, just as he reached his car, Colin's cell phone rang. He breathed a sigh of relief as Jessica's number appeared on the tiny screen.

"Hello?"

"Colin?" Her voice broke immediately, and he braced himself for the worst. "My grandmother. . ."

He listened to the rest with an aching heart. *Lord, help her. Give her strength.* The more she spoke, the more he found himself wanting to hold her—to tell her everything would be all right. After giving him funeral details, she paused for a breath.

Colin finally felt free to share his heart. "Jess, I want you to take your time. Stay with your family as long as they need you."

"But we have a show in eleven days." Her voice broke again.

"That's not important. The most important thing now is to be there for your mom. She needs you. I can handle the kids."

She began to cry in earnest now. "I–I miss. . .my kids. But don't tell them what's happened. Please. I don't want to make them sad."

How does she do it? She's thinking of the children when she should be thinking of herself. "Jessica, don't worry about the kids. They're doing great."

"They are? Do they miss me?"

"Yes, of course, but our rehearsal today went well."

"What about the costumes?" She sniffled, and Colin tried to picture the look on her face.

"All done. The costume department came through, as promised. Jeffrey Weaver had a small problem with his robe. Too short. Other than that, everything looks great."

Jessica sighed. "I wish I could have seen them. I'm sure they were adorable."

"You'll see them when you get back," he said. "In the meantime, get as much rest as you can and spend some time with your folks. Just keep me posted. I've been worried about you."

"You—you have?"

"Well, not really worried. Just concerned. I. . ." Suddenly Colin knew what he wanted to say, though the words rocked him to the core. He wanted to say, "Don't you know how much I care about you, Jessica? I want to be there, to walk you through this. I want you to rest your head on my chest again and let me tell you everything's going to be okay." *Where did that come from?*

"Colin? Are you still there?"

"I, uh—I'm here. I miss you, Jess. And I'm praying for you. But I want you to feel free to take your time." *Oh, but please don't take too much time. I miss you so much already.*

"Okay. Once the funeral is over," she said and sniffled again, "I'll spend some time with my mom. I'll probably come back next Sunday night."

"If you're ready."

"If I'm ready." Her voice seemed to change a little. "I'm so sorry, Colin, but I'm going to have to skip the performance at your church. I hate to let you down, but there's so much going on right now, I just don't think I could handle one more thing. Can you find someone else?"

"I'm sure I'll find someone," he said. "Please don't think a thing about it."

Jessica sighed. "Thanks for understanding. Oh, and, Colin. . ."

"Yes?"

"I just want you to know how much I appreciate you.

You've been such a great friend to me. I didn't realize how much I've come to depend on your friendship. I don't know what I would have done without it. I really don't."

"It's easy to be your friend." His heart suddenly swelled with emotion.

"That's so sweet. I appreciate that more than you'll ever know. And I'm so grateful for everything you've done—everything you are doing."

"I love you, Jess." Where the words came from, he had no idea. "And I'll keep praying. For you, your mom, and everyone down there."

A long silence greeted him, followed by a hushed, "You're awesome."

"Good-bye, Jess."

"Good-bye."

As soon as the line went dead, Colin suddenly felt as if he would be sick.

❧

I love you, Jess.

All afternoon long Jessica pondered Colin's words. His statement, though hurried and clearly impulsive, had truly left her speechless. Surely, he meant he loved her as a friend. However, the more she thought about it, the less sure she felt. *Lord, have I said something, done something to lead him on or give him the wrong idea? I love Nathan.*

For some reason, Jessica's thoughts immediately shifted to an earlier conversation with her grandmother, the day she had first tried on wedding dresses. "You can force something to fit," the precious older woman had said, "but that doesn't make it right. Living with something that's uncomfortable or 'not quite right' is never a good thing."

Sorrow overtook Jessica, and she crumpled to her knees in a haze of tears.

seventeen

"Is it always this cold in December?" Jessica asked her mother on the Wednesday afternoon following her grandmother's funeral.

"I don't ever remember a December this chilly." Laura Dougherty pulled her sweater a little tighter and continued to pace the room, as she had done for days now. The week had been a whirlwind of activity, and none of the pieces of the puzzle seemed to be coming together for any of them quite yet. The continual throng of people had brought some sense of comfort, but it felt good—really good—to finally have some time alone to grieve.

"Mom, you've got to stop," Jessica said. "You're going to wear yourself out."

Her mother shook her head. "I'm just thinking."

"About?"

"Something your grandma said to me a few days before she passed away." Laura's voice broke, and she paused for a moment. "She—she told me to follow my dreams, not to let anything stop me."

"She said the same thing to me a few months back," Jessica replied. "That's odd."

"That is odd." Laura paused. "Funny thing is," she continued, "my dream—the one I've put on hold for so many years now—is to open a bookstore. One of my own. I had almost forgotten."

"Right." For as long as Jessica could remember, her mother had longed to have her own shop. For years, she had worked in a large bookstore, but all along she had held on to the dream of one day becoming a proprietor herself.

"The oddest thing has happened. I don't know if it's just a coincidence or if God is at the center of it."

"What, Mom?"

"Madeline is selling the shop. She's moving off to Abilene to be near her parents."

"Really?" Jessica had known and loved Madeline from the time she was a preteen. If she left the store, everything would change. Of course, everything was already changing—and so quickly, too.

"I'm just wondering if your grandmother's words of advice were in some way—I don't know. . . ."

"Prophetic?"

"Not to overspiritualize, but yes."

"It is a little strange, Mom," Jessica confided. "Like I said, Grandma had a similar conversation with me awhile back—about following my dreams. That's why I decided to go to Dallas when I did."

"You're kidding. Your grandmother had something to do with your decision to move?"

"She had everything to do with it." Jessica wrung her hands together and formulated her words. "And it was the right choice. I haven't regretted it for one minute. It's not that I don't miss you guys. I do. And I miss the children at church, too. Of course, from everything I've heard, they've been too busy to miss me much."

"That Mrs. Witherspoon," her mother said with a smile. "She's a pistol."

"I know. I heard all about her from Grandma the last time I was in town. She's having a ball with those kids."

"Their Christmas show is this weekend." Laura's face lit up. "Will you be staying?"

"Yes. I'll be here 'til Sunday night," Jessica explained. *Colin, I'm so sorry I won't be able to sing at your church like I promised.*

"That's great, honey. It's been so good having you here." Her mother's eyes watered once again, and Jessica embraced her.

"I hate to leave at all, Mom, but I really need to get back so I can get to work. We've got a show of our own next week, and my kids are missing me. I've already talked to Colin three times this week. He says they're going through withdrawal." She stopped to reflect, then drew a deep breath. "I miss my students, Mom. I miss Dallas. I miss the opera."

"Is that all?"

"What do you mean?" Her heart lurched.

"I'm just wondering if you have the same sense of loss for Nathan when you're up there. He's the only person you haven't mentioned." Her mother's face reflected more than just a passing curiosity.

"Haven't I?" Jess paused as she thought back over the conversation. "Of course I miss him. I love Nathan."

"I know you do, Jess," her mother said, "and I'm happy you've had some time together over the past few days. But you two don't seem to be struggling through this separation as much as I anticipated, that's all. I'm not trying to pass judgment. Just wondering. Are things—I mean, is everything okay between you two?"

"We're fine. We're just so busy. Not that I regret the busyness." *If you only knew, Mom. I love it. In fact, I don't know when I've ever been happier.*

"I'm thrilled for you. I really am."

For a moment, the two women sat in silence. Jessica picked up a photo of her grandmother and examined it closely. "Everyone tells me I resemble her," she whispered.

"Not just physically." Her mother gave an assuring smile.

Jess held the photo a little closer. "What do you mean?"

"Your grandmother has—I mean, had—a lot of spunk. Not rebellion, just tenacity. It got her in trouble when she was younger. I've heard lots of stories about her antics. But mostly

I've heard about the efforts she went to, to make sure everyone got a fair shake, especially the underdog."

"Wow. I am like her then."

"Be proud of that, honey."

Andrew entered the room and shifted her mother's attention in a different direction, but Jessica couldn't seem to stop thinking of what she had just been told. *If I'm like my grandmother, there must be some reason. I need the same tenacity in my work and in my relationship with Nathan.* In her heart, Jessica vowed to rekindle the romance with her precious fiancé. He was worth it.

They were worth it.

Later that evening Nathan stopped by for a much-anticipated visit. After a quiet dinner with the family, he and Jessica took a walk to the neighborhood park, as they had done so many times over the years. Bundled in heavy coats and locked arm in arm, they talked. About everything. Missing each other. School. Work. Insecurities. Jealousies. And so much more.

With words of hope whispered in each other's ears, the excited couple reestablished feelings and committed to work harder on their relationship. The joy of planning their wedding took root again, and Jessica made herself a promise to do anything and everything to make this thing work.

ða

I love you, Jess. Colin still felt a little queasy as he contemplated the words he had spoken less than a week ago. Where had they come from? Why couldn't he seem to control them as they poured forth from his mouth?

"Jessica." Even as he whispered her name, joy flooded Colin's heart. *Lord, take care of her in Houston. Bring her back safely this weekend. Give her wisdom about the music. If she's supposed to stay in Dallas long term. . .*

Colin stopped his prayer immediately. *She's like a sister to me,* he reasoned. *I brought her to Dallas, and I feel a need to take care of her. That's all.*

Is that all?

Of course that's all. She's engaged. She'll be another man's wife soon. I need to focus on my own love life. Even as the thought drifted through his mind, an idea occurred to him, one he could not ignore. He picked up the telephone and nervously dialed Katie's number. *Keep your cool.*

When she answered with a cheery "hello" he almost hung up but somehow forged ahead with the words fresh on his mind. "Katie?"

"Yes?"

"I have a huge favor to ask. Feel free to say no." He went on to explain the predicament he now faced at church: Jessica had agreed to sing "O Holy Night" this coming Sunday morning but couldn't make it due to her grandmother's death. Would Katie be interested in singing it, instead?

"Oh, Colin! I'd love to. I'd be honored." Her excited response both relieved and impressed him. And why not? Katie professed a genuine love for the Lord. Besides, she had an amazing voice. She would blow the choir away. And Ida would be thrilled to learn that he had actually located a vocalist worthy of the coveted solo.

All the way to church, Colin thought about Katie. Truth be told, he had grown quite comfortable around her, perhaps even more so than he had been willing to admit to himself. Their evening together at the Italian restaurant had been truly enjoyable. In spite of the crowd, they had managed to find a table apart from the others, where they had visited at length. Her sense of humor amazed Colin. *Why didn't I ever notice it before? She's been such a blessing and she's been so patient with me. All this time, she's waited to see if I would show an interest in her.*

Am I interested in her?

Colin paused at a red light and gave himself over to the what-ifs in his love life. *Father, if Katie is the one You have in mind for me, please open my eyes—and my heart—to the possibility. Otherwise, Lord, please shut the door.*

Firmly.

The choir settled in for their final rehearsal a short while later, and Colin grinned with pleasure as he introduced a blushing Katie to thirty curious onlookers. When she opened her mouth and began to sing the beautiful carol, Walter very nearly dropped his teeth. The others sat in stunned silence. When she finished the song, the entire group rose to their feet and shook the room with their applause.

All but Ida. The elderly woman sat, arms crossed, in her chair with a skeptical look on her face. Clearly, she had issues with Katie. Jealousy, perhaps? As he moved forward with the rehearsal, Colin couldn't help wondering what thoughts his fiercest advocate held captive in her silence.

He didn't have to wonder long. As soon as everyone left for the night, Ida approached him in the church foyer. "Wrong girl."

"Excuse me?"

"That's not the one I've been praying for."

"I'm not sure I understand, Ida. Not the right one to sing your song?"

"Not the right one for you to marry," she explained.

"Who—who said anything about marriage?"

"Don't waste your time on the wrong girl," she huffed.

"Ida."

She left the foyer, muttering all the way. "Don't know why I bother to give my opinion. No one ever listens to me anyhow."

Colin shook his head in disbelief and turned toward the door. He drove home in dazed silence, trying to sort out his jumbled thoughts. *Lord, is this Your answer? Is Ida Your mouthpiece?* He could not seem to quiet his aching heart. For some reason, every time Colin tried to focus on Katie—her voice, her charm, her beauty—he could only hear Ida's firm voice, laced with irritation. *That's not the one I've been praying for. Don't waste your time on the wrong girl.*

eighteen

When Jessica arrived in Dallas the following Monday morning, she scarcely had time to collect her thoughts before finding herself in a musical whirlwind. The children met her with nervous anticipation. Colin greeted her with news of an additional performance opportunity. He assured her it would only take place if she felt up to it. She convinced him she could handle it. No problem.

However, with the deadline for the first show looming, Jessica had to wonder if she had taken on more than she could handle, both emotionally and physically. She found herself irritable and exhausted much of the time, and the children seemed to bear the brunt of her frustration. *I've got to try harder.*

With just a few days left before their performance, Jessica fought to give them her undivided attention. Try as she may, however, she couldn't seem to see past the fog of grief. Many times she found herself picking up the cell phone to call Nathan. He talked her through each moment in his usual practical way, and Jessica realized she missed him more than ever before. For the first time since arriving in Dallas, she truly felt torn between both worlds.

And yet she had little time for such confusion. The children's first performance of *Amahl and the Night Visitors* was upon her before she knew it. The excited youngsters sang their hearts out at several community functions in the two weeks prior to Christmas. Their final show would be held in two days on the big stage at the Met. They could hardly contain themselves as the big day approached. Jessica felt a little unnerved, as well. There was much at stake, after all. Several dignitaries from the city would be in attendance, as well as opera patrons and sponsors. This would be an awesome way to show off the new children's chorus and place the program in good standing for the upcoming spring season.

But Jessica couldn't stop to think about the spring right now. She just had to make it through this cold, hard winter— one day at a time. Though the weather had warmed a little, her heart remained in a frozen state, unable to thaw. Grief held her in its tight grip.

Many times Jessica stopped mid-sentence as something would remind her of her precious grandmother. A word. A smile. A warm embrace. Someone would mention something silly—like pizza—and she would burst into tears. Jessica found herself unable to let go of this woman who had meant so much to her. *Lord, I'll never let go.*

And yet, she must shift her attention to the children. They needed her, especially now. In the same way her grandmother had always been there to offer courage and support, Jessica now found herself having to give pats on the back and whisper words of comfort and advice. The children looked up to her with admiring smiles, and their hopeful faces lifted her spirits when she needed it most.

On the night of the big show, Jessica dressed in a new gown—a burgundy, ankle-length chiffon. When she arrived at the theater, she found the children in a state of nervous panic. Many seemed irritated or even physically ill. She recognized the signs of stage fright all too well. She asked Colin if he felt comfortable starting off the evening's festivities with prayer, and he never hesitated. The kids, dressed in biblical attire, formed a circle and allowed him to pray a rich, heartfelt prayer for the evening ahead.

Then the curtain went up. Jessica watched from the wings as the children she had grown to love sang joyfully. *Was it really just a month ago I stood on this very stage myself? How amazing to think these children will have the same opportunity. Lord, don't ever let them forget how special this is. And thank You, Lord, for letting me be a part of this. I can never thank You enough.*

Every now and again her gaze would drift to the auditorium, and she would strain to locate Nathan. He should be sitting in the third row—somewhere near the middle of the theater. *Ah. There he is.* The young woman to his left looked strangely familiar, and Jessica realized, with an odd sense of betrayal, that Kellie was seated next to her fiancé. Why should that bother her? She was a good friend, after all. It was only natural they would sit together. In the meantime, she must stay focused on the children.

When the curtain came down after the final song, Jessica cried like a baby. All of her pent-up emotions of the past two weeks came tumbling out. In order to avoid the children's curious stares, she pressed her way beyond the crowd to the props area. Here, she could be alone to think, to pray. Her thoughts were a jumbled mess. Between snatches of memories about her grandmother, she found herself facing inevitable questions about her relationship with Nathan. In spite of their recent conversation, she still felt something was amiss, though she couldn't quite put her finger on the problem.

"Jessica?" She looked up as she heard Colin's voice. "Are you okay?"

She nodded. She quickly dried her eyes, determined not to let him see into her heart. *I don't need to be sharing my emotions with anyone except Nathan. It would be wrong.* She quickly dismissed herself to the foyer, where she congratulated the children and visited with their excited parents. One by one, they thanked Jessica for her work. Many shared, through tears, the difference this program had made in the lives of their family. *Coming to Dallas was not a mistake. I would have missed all of this.*

As she made the rounds from child to child, parent to

parent, Jessica couldn't stop wondering about Nathan. *Why isn't he here? Did he forget we were supposed to meet after the show?* She finally excused herself from the joyous crowd and made her way to the theater. There, in the third row, Nathan and Kellie stood, completely engaged in a lively conversation. Jessica approached cautiously, trying to squelch the feeling of betrayal that now gripped her.

"Nathan?"

He turned to her, a wide smile on his face. It seemed to diminish a little when their eyes met. "Jess. Are you ready to go?"

"Yes. I've been waiting in the foyer," she explained. "Did you forget?"

"I'm afraid that's my fault," Kellie said with little giggle. "I had a financial question for him. I've been thinking about getting into day trading and thought he might have some advice."

"I see." Jessica rolled her engagement ring around her finger and eyed her fiancé for some sign of response. When he said nothing, she asked, "Did he?"

"Did he what?" Kellie's lips curled up in a cute grin, and Jessica noticed for the first time how truly adorable her neighbor was.

"Did he have any advice for you?" she asked.

"Oh yes!" With an admiring smile, Kellie dove into a detailed explanation of Nathan's words of wisdom.

Jessica couldn't seem to focus on Kellie, however. Her gaze remained fixed on her fiancé, who hadn't seemed to notice she was still in the room.

❧

From the stage, Colin looked out across the near-empty auditorium with curiosity. Jessica, Kellie, and Nathan stood just a few yards away. For some reason, he couldn't help thinking of Katie's whispered confession over dinner that night at the restaurant. *Kellie is crazy about Nathan.*

But what about Jessica? Where did that leave her? Colin had to wonder if she knew about Kellie's feelings. She didn't need to be hurt, especially not now. It wouldn't take her long to figure things out.

Colin felt a little sick as Jessica watched Kellie toss her blond hair. Her giggle bounced across the room. *Jessica looks upset. Should I say something, do something?* He looked at Kellie once again, wishing above all that she didn't resemble Katie so much. That only served to complicate his already confused feelings.

Right now, Colin had to confess, he only felt an overwhelming need to protect Jessica, to keep her from being hurt. *She's been through too much in the past few weeks.* He left the stage and slowly walked toward their row, approaching from an angle that gave him clear access to Jessica's expression. By the time he came up behind the group, there was little doubt in his mind about where things stood. Her beautiful green eyes overflowed with the pain of betrayal, though she continued to paint on a quiet smile. *I know what you're thinking, Jessica Chapman. Go on and admit it. He's hurting you. Right now.*

And Colin wanted to hurt him right back. *Stop it. This isn't your battle. And you don't know for sure that Nathan is to blame for this.*

He managed to catch Jessica's gaze and silently whispered, "Are you okay?" She nodded, but a lone tear slipped out of her right eye. Then he spoke. "Hey, everyone."

"Oh, hi, Colin!" Kellie turned with a gasp. "You snuck up on us. I didn't even see you there."

"Sorry. Didn't mean to scare you." He tried to gauge Nathan's expression. "What did you guys think of the children's performance tonight? Didn't Jessica do an amazing job with those kids?"

"Amazing," Kellie echoed.

"She's great." Nathan reached out and gave Jessica's hand a squeeze, then dropped it almost immediately. This did not go unnoticed.

"So, what's the plan now?"

"Oh," Jessica said, "Nathan and I have a quiet dinner planned. We're going to that new Greek restaurant on Stanton."

"Great place. One of my favorites." Colin nodded.

Jessica reached for Nathan's arm. "Well, I guess we'd better be going now. It's been a long night, and I'm tired."

Nathan extended his hand in Kellie's direction. "It was good to talk to you again. I'm sure we'll be seeing each other."

"Oh, of course." Her eyes, lit with excitement, spoke of her hope for future visits.

Colin didn't miss a thing. *How is Jessica taking this? She looks frustrated. No, she just looks exhausted.* He raised his hand to wave good-bye as the couple turned to leave. "Good night, you two."

Jessica muttered a quick good night. Nathan, however, simply nodded in his direction and kept walking.

nineteen

Christmas came and went, and before Jessica knew it, the New Year crept in. She spent the first day of January back in Houston with her family. A cloud of grief still hung over the group, and the usual cheerful exchanges did not take place. No countdowns. No parties. No celebrations. Instead, the day passed uneventfully. Even Nathan seemed oddly distracted. His quietness concerned her, and she tried to use her most cheerful tone when they talked, but something just felt. . .

Off.

That's the only word Jessica could use to describe how things were going. In spite of their earlier conversations, in spite of her attempts to make everything better. She tried to put her feelings of anxiety to rest, but they would not be quieted. In her heart, Jessica knew that something had changed, though she could not bring herself to voice the words. Instead, she tried to reason with herself. *I can make this work. I just have to stay focused.*

But staying focused wasn't easy, especially in this somber crowd. Jessica tried to serve as the cheerful one, often attempting to shift the conversation in lighter directions, but they would not be moved. Her mother melted into a pool of tears on several occasions, and Buck sat silently in the recliner, watching a muted television screen. Andrew made himself at home in the kitchen, fixing snacks and offering food to anyone who ventured near. Kent stayed away. A lot.

Jessica couldn't force herself to leave; though in her heart, she already longed to be back in Dallas—where a new season of music would soon kick off. Both the children's chorus and the adult company would dive right into auditions for spring productions, and the anticipation was almost overwhelming. Every time she thought about her life apart from her family, she felt guilty. Every time she thought about leaving Dallas in three months and giving up her dreams, she felt even worse. How could she pretend nothing had changed when everything had shifted into neutral?

For days, she swung between lethargy and bouts of nervous energy. Some mornings, she could hardly pull herself out of bed. Other days, she spent countless hours in a cleaning frenzy, doing everything she could to help her mother. She washed draperies, swept corners, and ironed shirt collars. And yet nothing seemed to bring a sense of relief. In her heart, Jessica truly longed to be home. With her children.

Nathan didn't seem to notice much change in her behavior. He spent a portion of the holidays with his family, and in the days prior to her leaving, seemed consumed with signing up for more classes at the college. In all, they barely had more than a day or two together. No time for wedding planning whatsoever, though the list continued to grow.

Jessica drove back to Dallas on a Sunday evening, the second weekend in January. As she pulled out of the Houston area, her spirits lifted immediately. Her excitement grew by the mile as she contemplated all that awaited her back home. Just three short months were left before her internship would come to an end. Jessica knew she must take advantage of the time. *God, thank You so much for giving me this opportunity. It's been the most awesome experience of my life.* Tears flowed down her face, and joy consumed her.

Joy, mixed with sorrow. *What will I do when it's over?*

Of course, she knew what she would do. She would become Mrs. Nathan Fisher, and he would make her the happiest woman on the planet.

Happy. When she contemplated the word, Jessica felt an

emptiness she had never known. *If this is happiness, why don't I feel. . .happy?*

Jessica sighed then allowed herself to think about her musical plans once again. The adult company would be performing a Gershwin review for Valentine's Day, and their springtime production of *The Bartered Bride* was sure to be amazing. And the children's chorus was growing—by five. She and Colin had been given permission to audition some new voices for the group, and she could hardly wait to look over the résumés.

Colin.

For some reason, Jessica couldn't stop thinking about him, and always with a smile on her face. *He's one of the greatest men I've ever known. And he's so awesome with the kids.* Guilt immediately consumed her, though she wasn't sure why. He seemed to know her better than almost anyone—except her grandmother, of course. He knew what kind of music she loved. He knew her favorite colors. He understood her passion for music and even shared her love for the children.

In short, everything about him brought a smile to her face, though that smile was always followed by an overwhelming sense of guilt. Jessica attempted to push all thoughts of Colin from her mind, knowing they were a distraction from the wedding plans. *I should be thinking about the wedding cake we're going to order next weekend. And I need to make a final decision about my bridal bouquet.*

And so she continually forced her attention to the wedding. With only four months left until the big day, Jessica knew she must hurry.

I don't want to hurry. I want everything to slow down.

Then the tears started once again.

❧

Colin pushed the fork around in the piece of chocolate turtle cheesecake, leaving an artistic imprint. He pulled the utensil back to examine his work. *Not bad.*

"Are you okay?" He looked up as Katie spoke. From across the table, he could see the concern in her eyes.

"I, uh—I'm fine." He dropped the fork onto the table with a *clink.*

"It's a brand-new year," she said. "A time for starting new things. A time for happiness."

"I'm happy."

"Right." She took a little nibble of chocolate before continuing. "You just seem a little quiet tonight. Something on your mind?"

Yes. I can't stop thinking about Jessica—can't stop worrying about her, wondering how things are going in Houston without me. Can't deny that I think she's wasting her time on that fiancé of hers. . . . Can't help wondering why you don't wipe that smudge of chocolate off your right cheek. . . .

"Colin?"

"I'm sorry, Katie. I really am." He shook his head in defeat. "I'm afraid I'm not very good company."

"You're unusually quiet." She wiped at her cheek with a heavy cloth napkin. "But I don't really mind. Just wanted to make sure you were okay."

"To be honest. . ." *How much should I tell her?* "I have a lot on my mind."

"About us?" Her hopeful eyes locked in on his.

"Us?" *How can she call us, us? We've only been on a couple of dates—both initiated by her. And I've certainly never done anything to—Stop it, Colin. Of course she thinks we're a couple. I've never had the courage to tell her what I really think: that this is a waste of time. That Ida was right. That I shouldn't—*

"Colin?"

"I'm okay. I promise. I'm just a little distracted tonight. I think maybe I'm coming down with something. To be honest, I haven't felt well for days now."

"You do look a little pale." Katie reached up and felt his

forehead. "Nope. Not hot."

"I don't have a clue what's wrong with me." He sighed and pushed his chair back from the table. "Something just feels off tonight."

"Maybe I should go."

He looked up from his plate with a shrug. "I don't want to hurt your feelings." *You're such a coward, Colin.* "Do you need a ride home?"

"No. I've got my car, remember?" She jangled her keys in his face, and he fought the impulse to be irritated at the little clinking noise they made.

"Right."

"Well. . ." She stood and reached for her purse. "I can tell you're not exactly yourself tonight. I'll just give you a call tomorrow."

"Okay. Sorry, Katie."

She left the restaurant with a dazed expression on her face, and Colin sat to finish his cup of coffee in silence. He tried to think about the upcoming auditions, tried to force his thoughts to the children. But all he could think about—all he wanted to focus on—was Jessica.

Guilt consumed him every time he remembered. *She's not mine. She's going to be another man's wife.* Then, just as quickly, the guilt was overshadowed by a tremendous sense of loss. Sorrow. She would be leaving in three short months. *Why do I feel so empty every time I think about losing her?*

For the children's sake, of course. They would miss her. They adored everything about Jessica. And why not? She had been sent from heaven to head up this program. For a season, anyway.

Colin took a sip of the coffee. Now lukewarm, it hardly brought him any satisfaction. He reflected on the fact that the children weren't the only ones who had gained an ally in Jessica Chapman. In his heart, he had grown attached, as well. *I've lost something that was never even mine in the first place. If I could only keep my mind on the music and just forget about her...*

Suddenly Colin remembered something his mother had said many months ago. How had she put it, again? Ah yes. "It's time you settled down. Found yourself a wife. Had a few kids. I mean, the opera is a good thing, but there's certainly more to life than music. It's one thing to follow your dreams; it's another to give up your personal life."

Colin shoved the fork into the cheesecake and stood to leave.

twenty

On the night of February 14, the Dallas Metropolitan Opera hosted a special evening of love songs—a tribute to George Gershwin. Just before the show, Jessica fought against her own emotions as she dressed. Nothing seemed to be going right tonight, though she couldn't put her finger on why. As she struggled with the red bow tie, she argued with herself. *Get it together, Jessica. What's wrong with you?*

In her heart, however, she knew. Something in the Gershwin tunes had struck a chord. Love—the kind she had been singing about—didn't exist. At least, not between herself and Nathan.

"But love isn't really just about feelings," she whispered as she twisted the bow tie into a knot. Still, she wished for a few feelings right now, especially since she had received the news that Nathan wouldn't be able to join her tonight. *Valentine's Day without my valentine.*

Somehow, it didn't hurt as much as she thought it would—and that worried her. They should be missing each other more. Shouldn't they? And why didn't the words of the love songs make her think of him?

Jessica stepped back to have a look in the mirror. Her black dress pants, white tuxedo shirt, and shiny bow tie made her feel more like a penguin than a vocalist. However, when Katie appeared at the door of the costume room dressed in the same attire, Jessica felt a little more comfortable.

"Are you ready? Snyder's a little snippy tonight." Katie's flushed face shone with excitement.

"I'll be right there." Jessica dabbed on a bit of lipstick and examined herself in the mirror. "I guess this will have to do."

She scurried across the backstage area and into the rehearsal room, where fellow vocalists sat, preparing for a final run-through of tonight's songs. As she entered the room, she noticed Colin's eyes. They sparkled as he turned to face her.

"You look great," he whispered.

She chuckled. "We all look just alike."

"No. Not you. You always stand out above the others."

"Maybe it's the red hair," she acknowledged with a smile.

"Nope. Not that. Although you do have beautiful hair. I think it's something else—something that comes from way down deep inside you. You're beautiful from the inside out."

Jessica marveled at the joy in his eyes. The depth. The caring. "You flatter me, Mr. Phillips."

"You make it easy, Miss Chapman."

She felt her cheeks flush and quickly moved to take a seat in the front row, amidst the other sopranos. Colin took his place in the third row. For some reason, Jessica's heart fluttered as he moved away. Something undeniable seemed to be stirring. *I don't get these same feelings around Nathan. Maybe I never did. Lord, what's wrong with me? What's wrong with my fiancé?*

As she took her seat and began the warm-ups, Jessica tried to focus on her wedding vows, which still needed to be written. Somehow, every time she rehearsed them in her mind, they came out sounding like Gershwin tunes. *I can't even think straight anymore.*

The music began, and Jessica's heart began to twist inside out. *I'm just lonely because Nathan's not here. I'm missing him.* But in her heart, she knew this wasn't true. Jessica finally began to acknowledge what she had probably known for some time now. She glanced across the room at Colin. The speed of her heartbeat nearly doubled, and she had to voice the inevitable. "I care about Colin," she whispered. "As more than just a friend."

The words nearly knocked her out of her chair.

All through the rehearsal, Colin fought a rapid heartbeat. He felt physically ill, though he couldn't quite figure out why. Probably just nerves. But he never got nervous—not like this, anyway. Why tonight? He joined the others as they traveled from the rehearsal room to the stage entrance. From here, he could hear the people in the auditorium and could almost envision their faces.

Almost. Funny. The only face he could see with any clarity was Jessica's. Her smile. Her whimsical pout. Her freckles. Her rich, auburn hair.

Colin traipsed behind the others to enter the stage. He took his place on the third row of the risers and waited for the curtain to rise. He had looked forward to tonight's performance above almost any other. The Gershwin music seemed to speak to him, perhaps even more so than the traditional classical music he had always loved. In his heart, he knew why. These songs voiced the very thing he had been afraid to speak.

Love.

What a wonderful, terrifying word. Love for a woman. Colin gasped as the revelation hit him like a freight train coming around the bend. The one thing he had been trying to avoid for months now seemed inevitable, and it very nearly knocked the breath right out of him. He had fallen in love with Jessica Chapman, and he must tell her.

He would die if he didn't.

From upstage right, Colin struggled to get Jessica's attention. "I've got to talk to her, or I'm going to explode," he whispered as the music swelled. *Father, if what I'm feeling, if what I know in my heart to be true is wrong, then stop me. Please. Settle these emotions, Lord.*

As they sang the familiar love songs, Colin watched the most beautiful woman in the world out of the corner of his eye. She stood out above the others, and he had voiced it well a little earlier. *It's not just her outer beauty, though she is prettier than the other women here. There really is something about Jessica—something that goes all the way to the core.*

Colin recognized her spiritual depth, that which gave her true beauty. She was by far the most amazing woman he had ever met. Probably the most amazing he would ever meet. *I don't deserve her.*

Oh, but I want her. And I want her to want me. He struggled with his feelings as the love songs continued. When his solo, "Love Walked In," began, Colin fought to swallow the lump that had grown in his throat. Love had walked into his life, and he could deny it no longer. He would deny it no longer. The words spoke more truth than he had ever been willing to face. He felt the depth of the words as they tumbled out of his mouth: "Love walked right in and drove the shadows away; love walked right in and brought my sunniest day. One magic moment and my heart seemed to know that love said, 'Hello,' though not a word was spoken."

I did know. I knew the minute I laid eyes on her. I knew that day back in Houston when she walked on that stage. Love walked into my life and changed everything. How could I have been so blind not to see what was in front of me all the time? Didn't I want to see? Guilt immediately seized him, and Colin begged the Lord to forgive him for these feelings.

And yet he didn't want them to end.

Colin looked her way as his song ended and her beautiful solo began. Clearly, Jessica favored her song above all others. "Someone to Watch Over Me," seemed to suit her—not just vocally, but in all other ways, too. Snyder had chosen Jessica to sing the beautiful female solo, and she did it justice like no one else could have. When she began the melancholy piece, the audience responded with cheers and whistles.

"There's a saying old, says that love is blind." She sang with her eyes closed. "Still we're often told, 'Seek and ye shall find.'

So I'm going to seek a certain lad I've had in mind." Colin silently willed her to open her eyes, to see the desperation in his own.

I'm that lad, Jessica. I'm the one you've been looking for.

As she continued on, he suddenly felt nauseous. Running from the stage seemed to be his best option. Instead, he drew in deep, calculated breaths and tried to focus. *How can I focus on anything but her?* Her gaze finally locked on his as she reached the chorus of the song. *Is it just a coincidence? She's supposed to be facing stage left, not stage right.*

Tears shimmered in her eyes as she sang—not to anyone else in the auditorium. Only to him. "There's a somebody I'm longing to see. I hope that he turns out to be someone who'll watch over me." Colin's heart leapt into his throat.

His gaze spoke a thousand words from across the stage. *I'm that somebody, Jessica. I want to be the one to watch over you. You'll never have to be alone.* But, then again, she wasn't alone. Nathan, her fiancé, provided an ever-present reminder. *If he's so in love with her, why isn't he here on Valentine's Day? Oh, but I'm so glad he's not here. If he had come. . .*

None of this would be happening.

Jessica continued to sing, and Colin found himself caught up in watching her—so much so that he almost forgot to join in on the chorus. *This is reaching a crazy point. I've got to do something, say something. I can't wait any longer. My heart can't take much more of this.*

When the song ended, he managed to get her attention and mouthed the words, "I need to talk to you." She nodded with a mixture of terror and curiosity etched on her beautiful face.

The final song of the evening drew to a conclusion with the whole group in choreographed formation, which, blessing upon blessing, placed Colin and Jessica side by side. As the curtain came down, he took advantage of the opportunity by grabbing her hand and whispering in her ear. "Jessica. I need to talk to you. It can't wait."

She looked up at him with a panicked expression and nodded silently.

"If I don't tell you this, I'm going to die." He pressed her hands into his own as he spoke above the excited voices onstage. "Remember that day on the phone when I told you I loved you?" She nodded, and her hands began to shake as he continued. "I didn't mean to say those words. I wasn't even sure where they came from, to be honest. But the truth is—I do love you." His words, rushed and passionate, astounded him.

She began to cry, and Colin gripped her hands even tighter. "I love you, Jessica. I've tried not to. I've prayed about it, worried about it—tried to forget about it. But I can't. I know that God brought you here—not just because of the music—but because we're supposed to be together. I prayed for a helper, and He sent me the best one on the planet."

"Oh, Colin." Her eyes filled with tears, and she squeezed his hands. Then, just as swiftly, she backed away and placed her hands over her mouth. "What are we doing?" she whispered. "This can't be happening." Thunderous applause continued from the other side of the closed curtain.

"It is." He pulled her to himself. "And it's too late to change anything. I love you, Jessica." And then, without planning a thing, their lips came together in the most orchestrated moment of Colin's life. The world seemed to disappear in a muddy haze as he held this gift, this amazing woman in his arms. The roar of love nearly deafened him.

Only when an elbow jabbed him in the ribs did he realize the roar came from the audience. When had the curtain gone back up?

For a second, Jessica looked as if she might faint. Her cheeks blazed with color. From stage right, Katie stared with her mouth hanging open. Several people in the audience began to cheer, and Colin realized, all too late, that he and Jessica had just exposed their feelings not only to each other—but also to the entire city of Dallas, Texas.

❧

Jessica tossed and turned in her bed, fighting the mixture of emotions that held her in their grip. *He loves me. Colin loves me.* The revelation brought wonder.

And terror.

I love Nathan. Don't I?

She wrestled with the truth, and it nearly strangled her in its grasp. *I don't love Nathan. Not like I should, anyway. But what do I do about that? Do I marry him anyway?* She twisted around in the sheets for nearly an hour before finally falling asleep. When she dozed off, familiar dreams swept her away to a place she recognized all too well.

Jessica saw herself on a stage, singing her heart out. She wore an exquisite, flowing dress in shades of cream and burgundy. To her left, a beautiful set filled the stage—an antiquated Italian city with houses, fountains, and cobbled streets. From inside the window of one of the houses, a man sang to her in a rich baritone voice, which resonated across the theater.

She responded to his words in Italian. Her soprano voice matched his as they joined together in harmony to complete the song. He disappeared momentarily, only to reappear in the doorway of the house. The tall stranger with dark hair moved toward her, never taking his gaze off of hers.

Only now did she recognize him.

Colin. I've been dreaming about you all along!

With great joy, he swept her into his arms and sang lovingly to her as he danced her across the stage. She found herself captivated by the moment and completely lost in his gaze. They seemed to mirror each other perfectly. From there, the dream faded to a dismal, gray haze.

Jessica awoke in a pool of sweat. She shook uncontrollably as truth overwhelmed her. Somehow, lying here in the bed with no one but the Lord to confide in, Jessica had to admit the truth.

I'm in love with Colin Phillips.

twenty-one

The week after Valentine's Day gave Jessica the time she needed to seek God's will concerning her love life. After much turmoil, she had to conclude that she could not carry through with her plans to marry Nathan. This revelation caused pain at first, but it had been followed by an overwhelming sense of relief.

Now she must tell her fiancé that she couldn't possibly marry him. Many times she ran through the conversation in her mind, trying to decide the best way to word things. And opportunities seemed to abound. She could have told him of her decision over the phone on several occasions. She could have shared the news as they chatted online. She could have told him any number of times in any number of ways.

But fear always stopped her. *He's going to be so hurt. He'll never understand.*

Besides, he always seemed to be more than a little distracted and even moody when they were together. Often, he didn't have time to talk at length anyway. His school schedule was tight, and his work commitments seemed to be growing daily.

Not that she had much time, either. The children's spring production was in full rehearsal, and the children offered hours of distraction from her woes. They were a chaotic delight, as usual. On top of their antics, Jessica had another amazing distraction. She had been offered the opportunity of a lifetime—a solo role in the adult spring performance of *The Bartered Bride*. With so much going on simultaneously, she had little time to contemplate the very real consequences of bartering her own romantic feelings.

In order to maintain a sense of openness before the Lord, Jessica made a commitment to cease any personal conversation with Colin. This proved to be quite difficult, in light of the hours they spent together daily, but she managed to avoid any private conversations and kept her thoughts and emotions to herself. Until she settled the issue with Nathan, she had no other choice. Everything was just too confusing right now. Instead, she made the whole matter an issue of prayer and committed her heart—and her future—to the Lord. Even if it meant spending the rest of her life alone.

By the time she drove to Houston the final weekend in February, Jessica felt more at peace about the whole situation. She knew the Lord would show her what to do. He could be trusted with her future. Hadn't He already directed her this far? Hadn't He given her the courage to come to Dallas to audition for the opera? He knew her heart, and He remained in full control.

In the meantime, Jessica knew she must confide in her mother at once. To wait any longer would be too difficult. Besides, she needed the assurance and the love of one who had already lived and loved so well. What better person than her own mother, who had always shared her heart so openly?

When she arrived home, Jessica took advantage of the first available opportunity to pour her heart out to both her mother and Andrew. She spoke carefully, thoughtfully, and didn't leave out a thing. She told them of her most recent revelation—that her feelings for Nathan were not what she had always thought. Though somewhat shaken, her parents seemed to take the news a little better than she had hoped.

"To be honest," her mother responded at last, "I'm not that surprised. In fact, I think I've known for a while. That's probably why I asked so many pointed questions when you were here last."

"It doesn't change your opinion of me?" Jessica wiped tears from her eyes as she spoke.

"Never." Her mother's eyes misted, as well. "I felt a little bad for putting you on the spot before, but now I know that God was obviously on the move. I can see that now."

"I'm so relieved. Thank you both so much for understanding." She looked at them with great appreciation.

"We trust your judgment," Andrew added. "And you know in your heart whether Nathan is the right man for you."

"It would be far worse to marry a man you were never intended to marry," her mother added. "I've known far too many people who did, and they struggled for years to try to make the marriage work. I don't want that for you, Jess. I want you to be able to have it all—the romance, the music—everything."

Then I have to tell them the part about Colin, too.

Tears flowed now, and Jessica freely shared all that had happened on Valentine's Day. At first, as always, guilt consumed her. But when she reached the point where Colin confessed his love for her, she couldn't help smiling. Her heart came alive, and her hands began to tremble. Even her lips quivered as she spoke the words, "I feel so bad about feeling so good."

For a moment, her mother didn't say a word. Then, when she did speak, her words startled Jessica. "I never thought I could fall in love twice in one lifetime." She took hold of her daughter's hands. "When your father passed away, I just accepted the fact that I'd be by myself for the rest of my life. I was so surprised when the Lord brought Andrew into my life."

"In a good way, I hope." He slipped his arm around her shoulders.

"A very good way." She patted him on the knee, and they hugged at length.

"You two are so romantic," Jessica said with a sigh. "I want a relationship like that. I really do. I didn't realize how much I wanted and needed that."

"Romance is very important," her mother said. "But love—real love—far exceeds any feeling or emotion. I know I don't have to tell you that."

"I always thought I knew what love was like." Jessica shrugged. "But now I'm not sure I know anything anymore. I feel like a little girl, all over again."

"That's not such a bad thing," Andrew said. "Just put your trust in God. He's still there."

"Just remember," her mother said, "God's methods don't always fall in line with what we expect. And He has an amazing sense of humor. Sometimes we forget that."

"I had almost forgotten. These past few months have had very few lighthearted moments. Between Nathan and myself, I mean. Up in Dallas, I've had lots of fun. I don't know when I've ever felt so fulfilled or so needed."

"I'm thrilled for you, honey." Her mother stood to give her a warm embrace. "Just promise me you won't make any rash decisions where your love life is concerned. These things take time, trust me."

Jessica wrapped her arms around her mother's waist. "I won't, Mom. Other than work-related things, I haven't even spoken two words to Colin since Valentine's Day."

"I'm not so sure that's good, either."

"I just haven't known what to say, so I haven't said anything. I think it's more important at this point to talk to Nathan and resolve our relationship in a way that honors God—and him. But I'm so scared I'm going to hurt him, Mom. I'm so scared." She dissolved into tears, and her mother held her in a warm embrace.

"You can't let that stop you from doing the right thing."

"I know." Jessica reached for a tissue and dried her eyes.

"One day at a time, honey. And one battle at a time."

As they wrapped up their conversation, Jessica finally felt free to breathe again. Now she could move forward with her life. Just as soon as she talked to Nathan.

She found her first opportunity to speak with him later that same evening. He arrived around six to pick her up for dinner. All the way to the restaurant, she sat in silence, planning her words. Just as they pulled into the parking lot, she turned to face him. "Nathan, I need to talk to you about something. Important."

"What's up, Jess?" He turned to face her as he pulled into a parking space.

"I need to tell you—"

At that moment, his cell phone rang, and he reached to grab it. "This will just take a minute. I'll get rid of them." He answered the phone, and Jessica tried, once again, to collect her thoughts. Unfortunately, his call lasted quite some time and seemed to be complicated. Something about one of his classes. Obviously something important. He remained on the phone nearly twenty minutes. When he finally hung up, she opened her mouth to begin again, but he managed to get the first word in.

"I can't believe that guy!" Nathan dove into a lengthy explanation of all that had transpired over the phone. On and on he went, sharing every detail. Something hurtful had happened at school. He had been victimized. Someone else was to blame. He had tried to make things right, but nothing seemed to work in his favor.

Jessica listened intently, but at some point in the story, she felt all of her courage drain away. As she and Nathan entered the restaurant together, she decided this would surely not be the night the Lord had in mind to break her fiancé's heart.

⋗⋖

I've lost her. The words ran through Colin's mind over and over again as he prepared the room for the children's arrival. *Why did I tell her? Why did I—how could I have kissed another man's fiancée? What's wrong with me? Why didn't I just wait and...*

And what? Live in misery without letting her know? Let her think he felt comfortable just being her friend when, in reality, he wanted to sweep her into his arms and hold her?

Forever.

But clearly, that would never happen now. She had gone back to Houston and, with the spring productions just a few weeks away, he knew she would only return for a brief time.

Then she'll be gone. What will I do without her? His heart twisted as if in a stranglehold, and he felt a lump rise in his throat. *Lord, help me resist these feelings. Don't let me give in. Help me do the right thing, Father.*

Colin pushed the lump back down and forced himself to focus on the children—on the upcoming rehearsal. With so much to do, who had time to worry about being in love anyway?

twenty-two

Weeks went by, and Jessica never found the right opportunity to share her heart with Nathan. She tried valiantly, but every time—every single time—something would happen to interrupt their conversation. Many times she found herself questioning both her motives and her feelings. Would it be better to hurt Nathan by telling him the truth or to marry him, knowing he wasn't the right man for her? If she married someone outside of God's plan, the consequences could be devastating for both of them.

And what about Colin? Jessica pressed all thoughts of him from her mind time and time again. But he would not go away. At night, in her dreams, he would reappear. In her thoughts, he would speak words of kindness to her. Jessica couldn't seem to shake his image, no matter which direction she turned. And working with him every day didn't help matters much. Continually, she was reminded of his warm smile, his love for the children, his passion for the music they both loved.

And his comments to her on Valentine's night.

Though the two never mentioned all that had taken place after that infamous performance, she could not stop thinking about his words, could not help remembering what it felt like to be wrapped up in his arms. It had felt so good, so right. But how could it be? *God, forgive me if what I'm feeling is wrong. I don't want to be out of Your will.*

But how could marrying Nathan be right, either? What good was a marriage that would only end in misery? She wouldn't be giving Nathan her whole self, even if she vowed to try with all her heart.

No, Jessica finally concluded, she could not marry Nathan. Even if God chose to close the door on a potential relationship with Colin, she could not—would not—carry through with the marriage to her fiancé. To do so would be to deny her heart and would be unfair to him.

But how could she tell him?

On the final weekend in March, she finally found the right opportunity to speak with Nathan and give him the dreaded news. He had agreed to drive her back to Dallas so they could have some time together. Alone. At first, she was thrilled at the opportunity. However, as the car pulled away from the curb, Jessica began to wonder if she could go through with this. *Lord, I need Your help. I don't want to hurt him. Help me, Father.*

Just as she opened her mouth to begin, Nathan spoke. "Jess, I need to talk to you."

"Okay. I need to talk to you, too."

"This is really important." He pulled the car off the road and gazed at her intently. "I, uh. . ."

Obviously very important. "Go ahead, Nathan."

"I need to tell you something, but I don't want to upset you. Really," he continued, "I guess there's no way to tell you this without upsetting you."

"What is it, Nathan?" Now her curiosity kicked in.

"I, um, I've had a lot of time to myself over the last few months."

"I know. I'm really sorry about that."

"Don't be," he said. "The time alone has given me a lot of opportunity to think—about who I am, where I'm going, all that stuff. I might have seemed stressed about being by myself, but God was using it to prepare me for something."

What is he going to say?

"I've had a lot of time to ask Him about the direction my life should be headed. And He's answered me. Pretty specifically, actually. In fact, I've been pretty amazed at all He's had to say."

"That's awesome, Nathan."

"Yes and no." He paused and shut off the engine. "What God has been sharing with me affects us both."

"Really?"

"I know I've been distant lately." His gaze shifted out the window. "I'm pretty sure that's been a subconscious thing. But I've had some issues to work out on my own—things that I couldn't tell you about."

"Like what?"

He turned back to face her. "Part of it has to do with school stuff—and my future. I've put out a lot of résumés over the past few months."

"Really? Any leads?"

"Yes, actually. I received a job offer last week. A really great one."

"Nathan, that's awesome. Where at?"

"Ironically," he said slowly, "in Dallas. It's with an oil and gas accounting firm. With my background in the industry, they felt like I'd be a good fit."

In Dallas? He's moving to Dallas? Lord, what are You doing here?

"That's what makes this next part so difficult." Nathan drew in a deep breath and shifted his gaze to the seat.

"Say it, Nathan."

"I don't want to hurt you."

"Just say it." A peace suddenly overwhelmed Jessica, and a sense of God's presence filled the car.

"I, uh, I've been thinking a lot about us, too," he whispered.

"And?"

"And I think—no, I know that we're—we're. . ."

"Go ahead." She reached out and gripped his hand.

"We're not supposed to get married." Now his words seemed rushed, and his gaze locked on hers as he forged ahead with a passion. "It's not that I don't love you, Jessica. I do. I've always loved you. But I don't think it's the same kind of love that a husband would have for a wife. I didn't want to hurt you, and I've been trying, for a while now actually, to make myself feel something I didn't really feel."

Jessica's heart soared. How could she possibly be happy with such terrible news? And yet, it wasn't terrible. "Nathan, you don't have to say another word."

"I don't?" He looked at her intently.

"No. I totally understand. And. . ." She swallowed hard. "I have to agree. In fact, I've been trying to tell you for weeks that I've felt the same way. I just couldn't bring myself to do it."

A look of sheer relief passed across his face. "Really?"

"Yeah." She grinned.

He rubbed at his brow. "It's been torture, hasn't it?"

"Yes," Jessica agreed. "And no. I wouldn't trade our friendship for anything. And God has taught me so much as we tried to force this thing to fit when it really didn't. And I know that there is a love between us—one we've shared since we were kids. Maybe we just misunderstood and thought it was the 'happily ever after' kind when it really wasn't."

"I never meant to hurt you," he whispered.

"I didn't mean to hurt you, either."

"I suppose it would have hurt a lot more if we had discovered this after we got married, don't you think?" He released her hand, and his eyebrows elevated slightly.

"Yeah."

"Jess, you're great. And I know God has big plans for your life. I'm sorry I haven't been more supportive. I'm not really into the opera thing as you know."

She shrugged. "No harm done. And I know the Lord obviously has some big things planned for you, too. But what do we do now? Do you still want to come to Dallas with me for the performance, or should we turn around and take you home?"

"Actually," he said and smiled, "I have an appointment with the new company tomorrow afternoon. I plan to stay for your performance then I'll fly back on the red-eye."

"I see." She leaned back against the seat and closed her eyes, rethinking all that had just taken place.

Nathan started the engine, put the transmission back into gear, and pulled out onto the highway. For the next two hours, he and Jessica had one of the best conversations they'd had in months—sharing their hearts, laughing, and marveling about God's goodness in their lives.

❧

Colin moped around his apartment in sheer misery. Weeks had gone by, and he couldn't bring himself to say a word to Jessica about his feelings. Right now, his heart felt like a lump of lead in his chest. *Lord, if this is love, I'm not sure I can take it.* A prayer arose out of his spirit and poured forth like water tumbling over river rocks. *What good is an occupation without a personal life? What if I worked all of my life and had no one to share it with, no one to come home to in the evenings?*

Colin could think of nothing worse than coming home to an empty house.

Except, perhaps, coming home to the wrong person in that house. Visions of Katie with those sparkling blue eyes tore at him, and Colin knew, beyond a shadow of a doubt, that Ida had been right all along. Katie wasn't the one he had been praying for, either. She was awesome. Amazing. Very nearly perfect, in fact.

Just not for him.

"How many people do that, Lord?" he whispered. "How many get defeated and settle for something—someone—less than the person You've selected for them?" The idea sent a shiver down his spine. "I'd rather be single forever than settle for the wrong woman. Help me, Father. Help me."

twenty-three

On the night of the opening for *The Bartered Bride*, Colin's trembling fingers fidgeted with his costume. *Just two more weeks and she'll be gone forever. Just two more weeks.*

He couldn't seem to stop the thought from rolling through his mind. Jessica would leave him—and the children—and would return to Houston to be married. She would become Mrs. Nathan Fisher in just a few short weeks.

And there was nothing he could do to prevent it.

Every time he considered the possibility of losing her, Colin felt weak in the knees. Children's program aside. Opera aside. He needed her. In so many ways, she fulfilled him. And yet, she did not belong to him. She belonged to another, and he would simply have to get used to that idea, whether it killed him or not.

Just one more time. If I told her just one more time how I feel, she might. . .

No. To say it again would only complicate an already chaotic matter. She clearly wasn't interested. She had hardly spoken a word to him in weeks, after all—and there had been plenty of opportunity.

Colin glanced at himself in the mirror once more before leaving the room. A light tap at the door interrupted his thoughts.

A stagehand spoke. "Curtain call in five minutes, Mr. Phillips."

"Thanks." He returned to fidgeting with the buttons on his shirt. Another light tap resounded on the door. For some reason, it irritated him, and he yanked the door open, ready to do battle—until his gaze fell on the beautiful angel on the other side. "Jessica?"

"Colin, do you have a minute?" Her eyes seemed to carry a new glow, an anxious glimmer.

"Just a few, actually. They've already called us for curtain." *This is it. This is the moment I've been dreading.*

"I have to talk to you," she whispered. Her eyes filled with tears immediately. "I wish we had more time."

"So do I." Now his eyes filled, as well. "But we're almost out of time, aren't we, Jess?" He reached for her hands and squeezed them.

"Yes."

"But I want you to know," he spoke with fervor, "that these last few months have been the best of my life. I don't know what I would have done without you. I really don't. You've been such a blessing to me. The children have fallen in love with you, and so have. . ." *No. Don't say it.*

"Colin, I have something to tell you."

"Curtain in two minutes, Mr. Phillips." The stagehand appeared again, this time looking quite anxious.

"Let's talk as we walk to the stage." Colin took Jessica's hand and led her to the backstage entrance. Somehow, with her hand in his, everything in the world felt right again. He could breathe again. He could sing again.

He could live again.

"I just wanted to make sure you knew—before you leave, I mean—how much it means to me that you came to Dallas in the first place." Colin looked at her intently. "I may never get the chance to say this again, but you've been a godsend. You've been a direct answer to prayer."

"Places, please!" the stage manager whispered with a firm hand on Colin's shoulder.

For a moment, Jessica looked as if she would faint. "I need to talk to you when this is all over," she whispered. Then, as she crossed the stage to take her place, her green eyes spilled over with tears.

She's going to miss the children. She's going to miss singing on this stage. She's going to miss. . .

The curtain lifted, and an audience full of spectators began to applaud wildly. Colin tried to focus on the show, tried to remember his first lines, but his heart, now torn in two, wouldn't allow it.

❧

By the time the show ended, Jessica found herself in a befuddled state of despair. Many times throughout the performance, she had tried to catch Colin's eye. Either he simply wasn't interested anymore, or he was trying to avoid her. At any rate, she must speak to him. Her heart couldn't wait any longer.

As the curtain came down that opening night, Jessica fought her way through the crowd to get to him. There, in the corner, he stood, surrounded by lovely prima donnas. They would have to wait. She had something to tell him. Something urgent. Eagerly, she pressed her way through the group and to Colin's side. She took his hand and squeezed it to get his attention. "Colin?"

"Jess?" He peered down at her with a look of eager curiosity.

"I need you."

"Excuse me?" His eyes began to twinkle with a bit of mischief, and the young women surrounding him took the cue. One by one, they began to scatter.

"I, uh, I need to talk to you. I have something to tell you."

"Right now?"

"Right now. It can't wait. Even a minute." Jessica couldn't seem to stop the grin from spreading across her face as she led Colin by the hand to the backstage door. With a triumphant swing, she thrust the door open, and they stepped out into the moonlight together. A night of wonder swept her into its trance. "Wow. It's beautiful out here." She turned in circles and gazed up at the sky, forgetting for a moment what had led her to this place.

"Sure is," Colin agreed. "But I'm a little distracted by something more beautiful right now."

"More beautiful?" She looked at him with heart racing. "You mean—"

"I mean," he said as he moved a step closer, "I can't see anything but you, Jess. I haven't been able to for months. I feel like a blind man staggering around in the dark, and yet I don't think I've ever seen more clearly. Does that make any sense?" He took her by the hand, and she immediately felt as if she might never be able to speak again.

When she didn't respond right away, his words poured out in a torrent. "Of course it doesn't make any sense." Colin raked his fingers through his thick, dark curls. "Nothing makes sense anymore, does it? I mean, on one hand, the world looks completely sane and normal. On the other hand, nothing seems logical anymore. I can't think straight. I can't sleep at night. And it's your fault. No, that's not right. It's not your fault. You haven't done anything. It's me. It's all me. I've fallen in love with you, and I don't know what to do about it."

Her heart leaped into her throat, and Jessica felt tears welling up in her eyes. "Oh, Colin." She could hardly contain her emotions and wanted to tell him—quickly—that she shared his feelings.

He took a giant step backward. "But it's wrong," he whispered. A lone tear tipped over the edge of his lashes, and he brushed it away with a vengeance. "You're not mine. And I can't feel this way. I'm breaking God's heart." He leaned against the brick wall in defeat. "I'm breaking my own heart."

"No." Jessica reached up and ran her fingers over his damp cheeks. "No broken hearts necessary. Not God's or yours. Certainly not mine." Now the smile spread from ear to ear. She could no longer hide her feelings. *I love this man. I have to tell him, or I'll die.*

"What do you mean?" His large hands suddenly felt as if they would crush hers.

"I have something to tell you. I've been trying to tell you all night, in fact."

"What, Jess?"

"It's just that. . .Nathan and I aren't—well, we aren't 'Nathan and I' anymore."

"Are you serious?" He let go of her hands and stared at her as though in wonder and disbelief.

"I'm serious. We decided, both of us, that we couldn't go through with the wedding. We realized that our relationship just wasn't part of God's plan for our lives."

"It wasn't?"

"No." Jessica swallowed hard. "After all," she whispered, "you can't marry one person when you're. . ."

"You're. . . ?"

"You're in love with someone else." Her gaze sought out his dark eyes in the moonlight.

"Do you mean that?" His voice soared with joy.

She nodded. Colin pulled her close, and as she laid her head on his chest, his heart raced in sync with hers. She knew, without a shadow of a doubt, that God had answered every prayer in one heartbeat.

"You are the most amazing thing that has ever happened to me." He planted tiny kisses on her forehead then lightly traced her cheekbone with his fingertip.

"I love you, Colin. And I'm so blessed. I don't know what I ever did to deserve you." Jessica choked back the tears that now threatened to overwhelm her. "But do you think there's any hope for us? Is it too late to start over again?"

With the moonlight guiding his way, Colin's lips found hers, giving his final answer on the matter.

epilogue

The costume director for the Dallas Metropolitan Opera appeared at the door with a gorgeous gown in her hands. "All of the alterations are complete, Miss Chapman." Her breathless words were rushed. "I'm really sorry it took so long. I just wanted this one to be perfect."

Jessica looked up from the mirror, where she had carefully applied an adequate amount of stage makeup. "Thanks so much, Amanda. I can't wait to wear it tonight." She examined the dress carefully, amazed at the intricate stitching and marvelous colors. "You did an awesome job. I can't believe how pretty it is."

"Thanks." Amanda grinned her appreciation. "You're going to look beautiful in it. Speaking of which, would you like some help dressing? All of those buttons might present a challenge."

"No thanks. I'm expecting help to arrive any moment." As the door to the room closed, Jessica turned to look in the mirror once again. Then, with her hands shaking, she stood and reached for the dress. Tonight's performance would be the opportunity of a lifetime—a chance to put to rest all prior fears and concerns. It would end all speculation and open doors to a beautiful and hopeful future. As she took the stage tonight, Jessica would realize the fulfillment of a dream that had begun years ago—a dream given by the Lord Himself.

A rap on the door interrupted her thoughts. She pulled her dressing gown tightly around her. "Come in."

Her mother peeked inside. "How's everything coming? Need my help?"

"Sure. I'd love that, Mom."

Her mother entered and smiled broadly as she faced the beautiful gown. "Oh, it's gorgeous, Jess! You're going to look amazing."

Jessica's anxious fingers tripped over the tiny buttons. "I don't know what's wrong with me tonight. For some reason, I'm a nervous wreck." She pulled the dress off of the hanger and slipped it over her head, nearly getting tangled up in the long, flowing sleeves. "I usually don't get preshow jitters," she said from inside the layers of chiffon, "but this is so different."

"What's that expression you theater people use? Break a leg?" her mother asked as she helped Jessica adjust the gown.

For the first time, Jessica noticed tears in her mother's eyes. "Right."

"Well, all I can say is, there's no way you could possibly sneak in an extra rehearsal for tonight's show. You have to count on God's ability to direct this one." She began the arduous task of buttoning the twenty-five pearl buttons that ran up the back of Jessica's dress.

"Mom, I can't tell you how happy I am." Jessica felt tears arise and immediately began to fan her eyes, hoping not to ruin her makeup. "When I think of how far I've come in the past year or two, I'm amazed. God has answered every prayer. Not exactly the way I thought he would, but He has definitely given me the desires of my heart."

"He's full of surprises, isn't He? But I'm not surprised the Lord has chosen to use you in so many ways, honey. And I know His blessing is on you. Tonight is just the beginning of many opportunities yet to come. I only wish. . ." Her mother choked back tears. "I only wish your father could have been here to witness this. And I can't help thinking of all the witty things your grandmother would have said."

"It's not the same without them." Jessica sighed as she held her mother in a tight embrace.

"No, it's not." The older woman stood back with a determined look. "But enough tears for us. You have to be on the stage in just a few minutes."

"How's the audience?" Jessica asked as she turned back to examine herself in the mirror one last time.

"Quite a crowd for an opening night performance. They're here because they love you, Jessica. And I love you, too. I don't know if I've said it enough, but I do. And I'm so proud of you. You've been such a godly example to all of the children here, and you've even taught me a thing or two in the past couple of years."

A knock on the door interrupted their conversation. "Miss Chapman?"

"Yes?" She peeked outside to respond to the stage manager.

"Curtain in five minutes. You sure don't want to be late for this one. They can't start without you tonight."

Jessica smiled. "You're right." She turned to face her mother. "You'd better take your seat, Mom. I don't want you to miss anything."

"Okay." Her mother held her tightly for a moment. "Oh, by the way—Andrew's waiting at the back of the theater. Do you remember where to meet him?"

"I remember." Jessica grinned and reached for the exquisite bouquet of red roses to her left. "And I can't wait."

❧

From upstage left, Colin waited. Tonight's performance would seal his future and write in stone every God-given dream upon his heart. Tonight—in just moments, in fact—Jessica Chapman would enter the stage and take his hand.

For the rest of his life.

From behind the Mediterranean backdrop, Colin waited for the music to begin. He sneaked a peek through the window, and his gaze fell on Nathan and Kellie, who sat, hands tightly clutched, in the third row. Their wedding, just weeks ago, had been a lavish, upscale affair. He and Jessica had attended with great joy.

Just in front of the newly married couple he located another old friend. Ida Sullivan sat in the second row with a look of pure satisfaction on her wrinkled face. Walter Malone was seated next to her, dressed in a suit that must, surely, be older than Colin himself. The elderly man leaned in to whisper something in Ida's ear, and she responded by smiling broadly. Colin took a second look. *Is he holding her hand?*

He barely had time to contemplate the matter. The stringed quartet began the introduction, and he swallowed hard as the familiar strain of music gave him his cue. His heart pounded in anticipation as he stepped through the doorway at the designated moment and began to sing. The love song he and Jessica had chosen was in Italian. Of course. Nothing else would have done.

He had rehearsed at length, though his nerves now kicked in, and Colin found himself barely able to get the first few words out. And yet he must continue. He would sing beyond the tears that now formed in his eyes. He would sing over the lump in his throat. He would sing the song of angels, and she would join him in a heavenly chorus, one that would require no interpretation.

As the words began to soar like ribbons on the wind, Jessica made her entrance from the back of the theater, stepfather Andrew at her side. The audience stood to their feet, and Colin could hardly contain the emotion that held him in its twisted embrace. *My bride!* By the time he reached the chorus, Andrew had released Jessica's hand, and she crossed the beautifully decorated bridge across the orchestra pit to join him onstage. By the time the second verse began, Colin's solo had become a duet.

&

Jessica fought back tears as she crossed the stage. Roman

columns, draped with tulle and twinkling lights, framed
beautiful Italian village, hand painted by the best set designer
Dallas had to offer. She hardly noticed it, however. She couldn
seem to take her gaze from the man she loved, the one th
Lord had dropped into her life when she least expected it.

Her grandmother's words of encouragement flitted throug
her mind rather unexpectedly. When had she spoken them
Ah yes—that day she had tried on wedding gowns. *You'
going to be a beautiful bride, honey, and that radiance is going
shine through like a light that can't wait to escape the darknes
because it will spring up from your innermost being.* For the fir
time, Jessica understood. From the very core of her being, sh
understood. *I love this man. Honestly and truly love him.* An
the light in her eyes must surely radiate the love she now felt.

His eyes seemed to dance with excitement, as well. Th
handsome baritone, tall and striking in his romantic Italia
apparel, sang to her in a voice she had only dreamed of. Sh
eagerly took Colin's hand and joined him in song. Thei
voices rose and fell, and emotion carried them through to th
end of the piece. Then, as the dramatic piece ended, the min
ister made his entrance.

Together, he led the two through the rest of the ceremon
With all her heart, Jessica vowed to love this man. To cheris
him. *You make it so easy, Colin.* She wiped tears of joy from he
eyes as he shared his heart openly and clearly for all to see an
hear. His handwritten vows seemed to ignite her heart and se
it ablaze. *Have I ever loved before? No. I've never known lou
until now.*

Now, at this very moment, all of her dreams ran crazil
merrily into truth. Into reality. Tonight, she would cling
the hand of this man God had given her and commit to rais
her voice alongside his for all of time.

Never again a chorus of one.

A Letter To Our Readers

Dear Reader:

In order that we might better contribute to your reading enjoyment, we would appreciate your taking a few minutes to respond to the following questions. We welcome your comments and read each form and letter we receive. When completed, please return to the following:

Fiction Editor
Heartsong Presents
PO Box 719
Uhrichsville, Ohio 44683

1. Did you enjoy reading *A Chorus of One* by Janice Thompson?
   ❑ Very much! I would like to see more books by this author!
   ❑ Moderately. I would have enjoyed it more if

   _____

   _____

   _____

2. Are you a member of **Heartsong Presents**?   ❑ Yes   ❑ No
   If no, where did you purchase this book? _____

   _____

3. How would you rate, on a scale from 1 (poor) to 5 (superior),
   the cover design? _____

4. On a scale from 1 (poor) to 10 (superior), please rate the
   following elements.

   ____ Heroine   ____ Plot
   ____ Hero   ____ Inspirational theme
   ____ Setting   ____ Secondary characters

5. These characters were special because?_____
   _____
   _____

6. How has this book inspired your life?_____
   _____
   _____

7. What settings would you like to see covered in future
   Heartsong Presents books? _____
   _____
   _____

8. What are some inspirational themes you would like to see
   treated in future books? _____
   _____
   _____

9. Would you be interested in reading other **Heartsong
   Presents** titles? ❏ Yes ❏ No

10. Please check your age range:
    ❏ Under 18   ❏ 18-24
    ❏ 25-34   ❏ 35-45
    ❏ 46-55   ❏ Over 55

Name_____
Occupation _____
Address _____
City_____ State_____ Zip_____

HIDDEN MOTIVES

4 stories in 1

Suspense, mystery, and danger pervade the four stories of this romance collection. As love blossoms for four women, threatening situations also arise where hidden motives abound.

Authors Carol Cox of Arizona, Gail Gaymer Martin of Michigan, DiAnn Mills of Texas, and Jill Stengl of Wisconsin teamed up to create this suspense-filled romance collection.

Contemporary, paperback, 352 pages, 5 ³/₁₆" x 8"

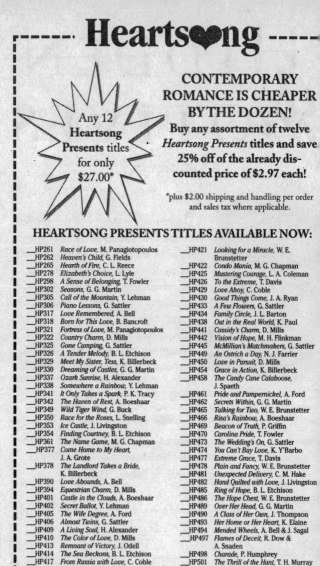

Presents

Great Inspirational Romance at a Great Price!

Heartsong Presents books are inspirational romances in contemporary and historical settings, designed to give you an enjoyable, spirit-lifting reading experience. You can choose wonderfully written titles from some of today's best authors like Hannah Alexander, Andrea Boeshaar, Yvonne Lehman, Tracie Peterson, and many others.

When ordering quantities less than twelve, above titles are $2.97 each.
Not all titles may be available at time of order.